"HAUNTING
AND
SEDUCTIVE."
—*Vogue*

"MASTERFUL...DEEPLY
AFFECTING."
—*New York Daily News*

"LYRICAL...
WILL APPEAL
TO READERS OF
*THE BRIDGES OF
MADISON COUNTY.*"
—*Publishers Weekly*

Donna Becker

Where or When

Anita Shreve

A SIGNET BOOK

SIGNET
Published by the Penguin Group
Penguin Books USA Inc., 375 Hudson Street,
New York, New York 10014, U.S.A.
Penguin Books Ltd, 27 Wrights Lane, London W8 5TZ, England
Penguin Books Australia Ltd, Ringwood, Victoria, Australia
Penguin Books Canada Ltd, 10 Alcorn Avenue,
Toronto, Ontario, Canada M4V 3B2
Penguin Books (N.Z.) Ltd, 182–190 Wairau Road,
Auckland 10, New Zealand

Penguin Books Ltd, Registered Offices:
Harmondsworth, Middlesex, England

Published by Signet, an imprint of Dutton Signet, a division of Penguin
Books USA Inc. This is an authorized reprint of a hardcover edition published by Harcourt, Brace & Company.

First Signet Printing, October, 1994

10 9 8 7 6 5 4

For Ozzie

Acknowledgments

To Claire and Ginger—who stood by me.

Existence permeates sexuality and vice versa, so that it is impossible to determine, in a given decision or action, the proportion of sexual to other motivations, impossible to label a decision or act "sexual" or "non-sexual." There is no outstripping of sexuality any more than there is sexuality enclosed within itself. No one is saved and no one is totally lost.

MAURICE MERLEAU-PONTY

One

$\mathcal{I}$ remember everything.

A kiss at the nape of the neck.

You said you used to have a dream. When we were children, you dreamed that the nipples of my breasts burst through the fabric of my blouse. And when we were grown, you said the dream came back to you, and you had not had it in all the years in between.

When we were children, we whispered words like novices at vespers. We were children and afraid to say the words aloud. I believe this gave us longings that would last a lifetime.

But that afternoon, what did I know of indelible connections?

It was a September afternoon, a Sunday afternoon, and I remember that it was raining. There were a hundred people in the wood-paneled library at the college, and a stack of books on a table by the door. Some friends were there, and my husband, Stephen. My daughter was not. I watched my husband gesture with his glass, embrace with a sweep of his hand (the wine spilling a bit over the rim) the entire room of people, as if he might still his own anxieties by becoming my most exuberant supporter. It was Stephen in a gray sweater and a blazer, who was standing by the table with the books—the books and that day's newspaper, with my own picture in an advertisement.

Earlier that day, when we had driven to the college, Stephen had been quiet in the car. The onion sets that spring had been washed away by heavy and unexpected rains. Stephen had missed one payment at the bank, might miss another soon.

It wasn't anything that Stephen had done or had not done. All the onion farms were going.

The farm that Stephen might lose was set upon the dirt. They called it "black dirt," a soil as black as soot. Each year, in the spring, when the water had receded, if the sets had not been washed away, the tender shoots sprouted up from the soil in perfect rows and turned the black dirt to a shimmery onion green.

But the farm was not mine. Never mine.

It was the first time there had been a party, though there had been other books, other collections. The book, as you saw, was a slim volume with a paper cover in a matte finish, a slim volume of some thirty poems. This book would gain little more attention than the others had, though there was the party this time and money for an advertisement, just the one.

For the picture for the advertisement, I had been asked to wear a black jersey, and at the studio the photographer had removed my glasses, had taken the clips from my hair and mussed it with his fingers. The result was a likeness, recognizable as me, though essentially dishonest.

At the party, I stood at the edge of a small room while people moved around and past me and sometimes stopped with a sentence or a word. I remember that my editor came up to me and said, in a moment of unwarranted optimism, a friendly unwarranted optimism meant to deflect attention from the fact of the disappointingly small printing, that this slim volume would change the direction of my life. And I had smiled at him as if I, too, might share this optimism, though I had thought then that my life would not change, not beyond the small, seismic vibrations of a child growing, of a house slowly settling into the soil, or of a marriage—in unmeasurable, infinitesimal increments—disappearing.

I am in disgrace now. Removed from a state of grace.

When you and I were children, we learned of death. It was in the inevitability of a final separation, a death against which we were helpless. And even as adults, leaving you was always brutal.

I always wanted to ask: Did your wife give you the leather jacket? Did you wear other clothes, a tie perhaps, a shirt, that she had given you and that I touched?

Toward the end of the party, my editor made a toast. When it was over, I looked up. Within the crowd, I searched for Stephen. He was by the door, his back against the wall, draining his glass.

I watched my husband set the glass upon the stack of books, leaving a wet circle on the matte finish of the top cover. I watched Stephen leave the party without a backward glance.

EVEN ON THE BAY SIDE, THE WAVES ARE SPIKING, SPITTING their caps off the crests. He likes it this way—hard and bright; these are the best mornings. The gulls, the rats of the sea, push against the wind, then swoop and dive for their catch. The old men are on the bridge, as they are every Sunday, braced against a railing that cannot last another year, even though he has been thinking this for years and the railing never gives. The bridge is wooden, nearly a mile long, the ride rattling in good weather, slick and treacherous when the spray freezes over the thick wooden slats. The bridge connects the mainland to a slender sliver of beach, and in the summer the bridge shakes under the weight of the Dodge Caravans and the Jeep Cherokees with their women and children, their beach umbrellas and blankets, their coolers of sodas and sunblock. But by now, the second week in September, the summer people have cleared

7

out, and Charles and the old-timers finally have the place to themselves.

Charles sails the aging charcoal Cadillac gracefully along the rough planking. He nods and waves at the men in their stained parkas, plaid jackets, and baseball caps, their shoulders hunched against the wind, watching their lines for a tug that looks slightly different from the pull of the current. He drives this bridge two, three times a day, takes the car each time to the end. Sometimes he gets out to cross the dunes to the ocean side, to look out toward Lisbon or Rabat, or to watch the fishing boats come in around the bar to the harbor, south of the bridge. At other times he simply sits in his car, listening to Roy Orbison, nursing a beer, maybe two, until it's time for his next appointment or to drive back to the house, where Harriet and his children seem always to be waiting for him.

Today they need milk for breakfast, and he knows he shouldn't have taken this detour. But the morning is too fine, he rationalizes, to have missed. Beside him there is the half gallon of two percent, a heavy Sunday paper this week, and a greasy bag of jelly doughnuts he has bought for the kids, although he knows that by the time he arrives home, his children already will have eaten a breakfast that did not require milk. Harriet will disdain the doughnuts, will not even open the package, will set them aside on the counter until, inside the spotted bag, they will grow hard around the edges and finally be inedible. Thinking this, Charles is determined to eat at least one, even though, as a rule, he doesn't like sweets. He parks the Cadillac in the small circle of blacktop that grows more circumscribed each year by the encroaching sand, takes a doughnut from the bag, gets out of the car, and walks toward the dunes, which prevent him from seeing the ocean side. He has on his jeans, a white dress shirt he's been wearing since Friday, and a black hooded sweatshirt over that. Unthinkingly, he has worn his leather shoes with the tassels, his dress shoes, and as he walks they quickly fill up with sand along the edges. He bites into the doughnut; the jelly squirts over his fingers. With his free hand he tries to remove his shoes and his socks. He licks his fingers; the sand is cold on the soles of his feet. How quickly the warmth leaves the sand in September, he is thinking.

The view from the top of the dunes is always worth the small climb. The sea is charged, yet still a vivid navy. Whitecaps appear and vanish like blips on a radar screen. He descends the dune and walks toward the water. The gulls hang motionless in midair, unable to make headway against the wind. Even the sand, a thin sugar above the crust left by high tide, echoes the spray off the whitecaps, stinging as it does against his bare feet. But it is the blue, a deep inexhaustible blue, which speaks to him of clear uncomplicated days, that stops him. He wants, as he always wants, to have it, to possess it, to take it with him, to take it out when he needs it. For he knows that by this afternoon, this particular blue will be gone—replaced by muted colors, grays or greens.

"Hey, Charlie Callahan. You takin' in the rays, or what?"

Charles turns to see the speaker, but he already knows by the gravelly voice that it is Joe Medeiros, a presence in town, a client. Joe made his money as a draggerman and looks the part: two-day growth of beard, a plaid quilted jacket worn so badly in the elbows you can see the polyester, stained chinos. One of Joe's front teeth is badly discolored. Medeiros is a man embarrassed by his teeth and consequently never smiles. Charles can smell the stale breath even in the salt air. He knows it's bourbon.

"Fishing?" Charles asks.

"Had my line in. Saw your car. Can't pull anything but pogies."

Charles waits, shoes in one hand, the other in the pocket of his jeans. He knows this won't be a casual visit. Joe is wheezing from the awkward climb up the dunes. Joe won't be interested in the view either.

"How's business?" Joe pulls a pack of Carltons from his jacket pocket, lights one away from the wind.

Charles shrugs, a practiced and familiar shrug. "Hanging in there. Same as everybody."

"You got that right." Joe exhales. The wind sends the smoke under his chin, into his collar. "Hadda sell two boats last week. Hadda give 'em away, I should say."

Charles looks down at the sand. Jesus Christ, he thinks, here it comes.

"So here's the deal." Joe studies the harbor as if searching for one of the boats he had to give away. "The fuckin' bank slashed my credit line. You know me, Charlie: I been doing business with Eddie Whalen with a handshake for years, and I've paid the bastard faithfully every month. And this is the reward I get."

Joe Medeiros coughs on the smoke or on his anger, hawks up a glob of phlegm to make his point, spits it onto the sand. "So I go down to find out what's the story with the credit line, and I find Eddie sweatin' bullets. Thinks *he's* going to get the boot now. The FDIC's been goin' over his stuff, and they're tellin' him now that he might of made some loans shouldn't of been made, you follow me. Fact is"—and here Joe Medeiros looks away, unable to meet Charles's eye—"the cash I was gonna use for the premium? I gotta have it for the mortgage payment. It's that simple."

Charles looks out toward Morocco. He has never been to Africa, nor even to Europe. He wishes he had the ability to banish Joe Medeiros from the dunes, make him disappear. He minds his Sunday morning invaded, the scene soured by the talk of business, the panic he doesn't usually feel until Monday's dawn beginning the slow crawl up his spine.

"Same old story, isn't it?" Charles says casually, as he has had to say too often in the past ten months. He is not surprised that the feds have been looking at Eddie Whalen's books. Eighteen months ago, Whalen was giving money away. Sign on the dotted line. As Charles and half the men in town had done.

"Stop by the office tomorrow or the next day," Charles says. "We'll talk. We'll figure something."

With his toe, Charles scratches idle markings in the sand. He knows he ought to have gotten Medeiros's premium up front. The $15,000 commission check would have paid Costa. Tomorrow he will have to call Costa, cancel the construction on the addition. And Costa is a client—Charles will lose his business.

Christ, it never ends, it seems.

"So when are the fuckin' banks going to have a dime to put out on the street? That's what I want to know," Joe says, looking at Charles now. The fisherman takes another drag, throws the cigarette onto the sand, business concluded. Small sparks from the lit end blow toward Charles's bare feet.

"The wife?"

Charles nods.

"The kids doin' OK? I gotta hand it to you, Charlie. You got the whole scene. Am I right?"

Charles hates this part, the denouement, the ingratiating banter after bad news.

"The kids are fine," he says carefully.

Another case shot. Charles fights the panic by looking out to the ocean, imagining the Azores. He focuses on a fishing boat trying to negotiate the gut in the chop.

"So I'm goin' back to my line. Probably snagged a shitload of seaweed." Joe turns as if to leave, then stops. "Listen, Charlie, I'm sorry as shit about this. You know what I'm talkin' about. I know you do. I don't ever forget how you drove out to Jeannette's. After Billy . . ."

Charles looks up at Joe. The fisherman's nose and eyes are running in the wind. Medeiros's son, dead before he was twenty-five, drowned off his father's fishing boat. Charles had sold Medeiros insurance on both his sons, and he remembers the drive out to Billy Medeiros's wife with the check. After he'd heard of Billy's accident (seven years ago at four-thirty on a summer afternoon, and Charles was in The Blue Schooner; the news had rippled down the barstools like a loose and slippery eel), Charles had done the paperwork at once, gone that night to the funeral home for the death certificate, cut out the obituary from the local paper, and sent the required documents in to the home office. In ten days he had a check, which he carried in the breast pocket of his suit coat up the steps of Billy Medeiros's small bungalow on the coast road. Charles had seen grief before—it sometimes went with the job—but never anything as bald as on that day. Jeannette, a small woman with thin dark hair, met him at the door, and at first he didn't recognize her. Her face was fish white, years older, and swollen with her pregnancy. Beside her was a daughter, not four years old, who sucked her thumb.

Charles remembers how he took the check from his pocket and handed it to the woman and how her face changed as she comprehended the meaning of the check, how she once again experienced the irrevocability of her husband's accident. And Charles remembers how Billy Medeiros's wife seemed to fold in upon herself, fold in upon the high soft moans that sounded to him almost sexual in nature and struck him as too intimate for witnesses. He recalls wondering what his own grief would sound like if Harriet died, recalls thinking guiltily that it probably wouldn't sound like Jeannette Medeiros's. He had stood helplessly, not knowing if he should touch Billy Medeiros's wife to comfort her, his hands seeming to float huge and useless in his pockets. Finally he had picked up the silent and frightened daughter and taken her out of the house. They'd gone for a Dairy Queen and a round of miniature golf.

Remembering that day and watching Joe Medeiros recross the dunes, Charles thinks again that his job is an odd one to have fallen into—and that is how it seems to him, something he has fallen into, wandered into, not chosen—a far cry from the seminary, though sometimes not. He has few illusions about how his job is perceived by others: an unwelcome (if often necessary) chink in the machinery, a job falling somewhere between that of a CPA and a tax lawyer, the occasional butt of jokes on late-night TV. Usually he thinks of himself as simply a businessman, a salesman with a product, a man who is better with people than he is with the paperwork. Though once in a while, on days when he is filled with hope, he likes to think of himself as a Life Agent, with all that the title, as metaphor, might imply—an agent for Life, an insurer of life, even a kind of secular priest—and he imagines his clients, an entire town of clients (his flock?), as motivated by love, buying insurance from him because they love a woman or a man or a child.

But inevitably there are the bad days, the ones when he wonders if he isn't after all only a paradoxical and unwitting harbinger of mortality.

Last Tuesday was the worst. Just the visual memory of Tom Carney sitting behind his desk makes him shiver involuntarily beneath his hooded sweatshirt. He looks out to sea, as if to shake off the memory, but it is in place now, and though he is watching Cole Hacker tack his Morgan through the gut, it is Carney that he sees.

Charles had pulled into Tom Carney's gas station at twelve-thirty, left the Cadillac by the pumps. A teenage boy with spiky black hair came out of the office.

"Fill her with special," Charles said. "Tom in?"

"He's in the office," the boy told Charles.

Charles walked to the office, opened the door. Tom Carney, an inch taller than Charles's six feet three, sat sideways to his desk, a desk littered with receipts, one greasy rag. Carney was bald already, had lost his hair early. The two men had joked about middle age: hair where you didn't want it, none where it was supposed to be. Carney's face, in adolescence, had been badly scarred by acne, and sometimes he still got pimples. Charles had told Carney that this was a hopeful sign— the man's hormones were still working.

Carney was smoking when Charles walked in, and his face was a grayish color that looked like fabric. On the desk was a Styrofoam cup of milky coffee, also grayish-looking, not touched. When he visited this office, Charles often had an impression of metal, as if the room and its entire contents were constructed of metal—metal walls, a metal desk, a metal chair—and this somehow was in keeping with the ever-present stink of gasoline in the air.

"It's right there," Carney said to Charles. Carney indicated an open letter with his hand. Charles remembered then that Carney didn't smoke; he'd given it up years earlier. Charles took the letter from the desk. Clipped to its top was a check. Charles read the relevant sentence.

He remembers a sensation of being buffeted—as if the air had been blown out of the room.

"Jesus Christ," Charles said softly.

Charles had gone to school with Carney, had played basketball with him, and the two boys had made it as far as the regional championships together. Then Charles had gone off to college and into the seminary, and Carney had stayed to work at his father's Mobil station. Carney owned it now; the father had retired. That was how Charles's business worked; he insured his friends, their referrals. Carney had held off for years, though, had had his children late. Usually it was the fact of the children that brought the new clients in.

Three weeks earlier, Charles had sent in Carney's application on a $300,000 policy, and he'd thought little of it until he'd opened his mail Tuesday. Carney's case was what the home office referred to as "a flat declination."

"Your client is unacceptable for medical underwriting reasons," the letter had read. "No further details are available. The initial deposit is being returned to the client with a letter of explanation."

Charles had been mildly worried for himself financially (another case shot); more seriously for Carney. Such a flat refusal didn't simply mean your client had high blood pressure.

Charles looked at Carney in his metal office. Through the window, Charles could see the boy replacing the cap on the gas tank, moving the Cadillac away from pumps. The boy's gestures seemed choreographed, dreamlike.

"I've got two kids," Carney said.

Charles held the piece of paper, read the sentence again. He wanted to say to Carney that there must be some mistake, but he knew it wasn't a mistake. The blood tests never lied.

"And my wife . . . I've got to tell my wife."

Charles put the letter back where it had been. He wanted to know how, but would not ask. He wanted to say he was sorry, but that seemed an insult.

"You want a drink?" he asked Carney.

Carney was quiet, wouldn't answer him. Carney's hands were large, had always been large. He'd been brilliant, fast with the ball.

"Let's get out of here, Tom, go get drunk at least," Charles said.

Carney was staring at a spot on the opposite wall. He shook his head slowly. "About five years ago, I had some encounters . . . ," he said.

Encounters. The word hung in the air. It was an oddly restrained and formal word for Carney to have used, and it didn't necessarily mean one specific thing or another, but Charles didn't have to know more.

After a silence, Charles had left Carney in his office, left the gas station. He'd gone to the Qwik Stop, bought a six-pack, and driven over the bridge to the beach. He'd drunk the six beers as fast as he could, on no lunch. It had seemed to him then that if he hadn't tried to make the sale, Tom Carney would never have known. It was illogical thinking, Charles knew, but he couldn't stop himself from making the loop. He'd thought of Portugal that afternoon, of emigrating to Portugal. He had wanted to be sitting at a café in the hot sun, eating braised octopus with Portuguese sausage and—for a change—looking out the other way across the Atlantic. He'd missed two appointments.

Charles watches Medeiros disappear behind the dunes, relieved to be alone again on the beach. Charles likes the bridge and the beach, and he thinks of the drive here as the "drive to nowhere." He imagines the drive itself, the drive alone even without its eventual destination, as a balm, a respite from the business in town. And sometimes, when he comes here and when he is absolutely certain he is all alone, he sings: show tunes, oldies from his youth, once in a while a current hit that had captured his imagination on the radio and that he has bothered to learn the lyrics to. He likes his voice—a good Irish tenor—and occasionally he wishes he could join a church, any church, just for the pleasure of singing in a choir, though immediately, when he has this wish, he thinks of having to endure the rest of the service or the mass, and his fantasy deflates. So he sings alone. Often, if he can, he brings Winston with him, his dog, his black Lab, and if he can get him going, he will sing too—a high, lonesome, off-key wail that drives the gulls crazy and almost always concludes with Winston bounding out of the car along the dark muck of the bayside, chasing the gulls and plunging into the frigid waters if need be.

It was why he'd bought the oversize Cadillac, a car

big enough, he thought at the time, for himself and his dog. (Charles thinks of himself as getting bigger too, with each passing year, as if life itself were causing him to inflate, though except for the occasional pound or two, he knows this can't be true.) There were other reasons as well for the purchase, all of them nebulous but of equal weight, the sum total of which urged him to make this uncharacteristically showy gesture. He'd driven a Cadillac in Milwaukee on a business trip, and the car had reminded him of the big cars of his boyhood, the mythic Bonnevilles and Chevrolets of his early teens. And when he'd come home from the business trip and passed the Cadillac dealership and seen the sign announcing the sale, he'd pulled in, knowing as he did so that he'd be seriously chastised if he bought such an ostentatious American car, by Harriet and by his friends and even by many of his clients, and somehow this had perversely pleased him, though not as much as turning in the Saab—that ever-present symbol of New England yuppiedom—had done.

Charles crosses the dunes twenty minutes behind Medeiros. He takes the bridge fast; by now, he knows, Harriet will have passed from merely impatient to tight-lipped. He reaches down in front of the passenger seat, snaps the cooler lid, brings a bottle of beer between his legs. With a practiced gesture, he twists the cap, inhales a long swallow. It's ten o'clock in the morning. But it's a Sunday; it's OK. His soul is not in jeopardy. Yet.

At the end of the bridge, the road forks. To the north is a tight string of low-rent beachfront houses, a wall of thin shacks that stretches along the coast to a power plant at the end of a rocky beach. To the left is High Street, residential until the harbor and the village itself. Here the houses are more substantial—two-story, wooden-frame homes with peaked roofs, most of them year-round. The yards are small, postage-stamp, some bounded in the chain-link favored by the first-generation Portuguese and Irish, others bordered by the hedges and white picket fences preferred by their children and the newcomers.

Sometimes now, driving this road, Charles imagines that there has been a war or at least a skirmish—something to explain the bombed-out landscape, the physical and psychic eyesore of stalled construction, additions that will never be completed and that now lie covered with torn blue tarps, condo complexes aborted even before the windows got their glass. Where once there were weathered saltboxes surrounded by sea grass, now there are abandoned foundations, signs that say No Trespassing—ugly, half-built concrete objects that mar the blue of the ocean. He passes such a sculpture, with its rusted girders pointed toward the heavens, and thinks of Dick Lidell. Two years ago, Charles sold Lidell a policy for three million, and when the home office wanted to look at Lidell's tax return, Lidell had shown four million five in cash. The man could have retired. Instead the four million five went into the Tinkertoy with its orange girders up on the hill, and Lidell, Charles knows, is now renting someone else's two-bedroom condo.

The stories are legion. Charles passes his office, a modest white Cape with dark green shutters. In the front, hanging from a wrought-iron post, is his sign: Charles A. Callahan/Real Estate and Insurance. Each year Harriet tends the garden around the front porch of the office and hangs a basket of geraniums on the post with the sign. It was Harriet who found the old wicker rockers at a garage sale, rewove them, and painted them green to match the shutters. The rockers have been on the porch for three years now, though no one ever sits in them. He hates passing his office, hates thinking of having to go to it in the morning. The building will be the bank's within a matter of weeks. He will have to move his business into his home then, a move that doesn't bear thinking about.

He knows, of course, that it was greed: an unfamiliar sin of boyhood, a ubiquitous sin of middle age, or so it seems to him now. But nearly as bad, he believes— almost as damning, almost as venal—was his carelessness, his recklessness.

At the time, the idea seemed to Charles like a certainty: All he had to do, Turiello explained, was take the equity out of the office, then leverage that cash into a one-third share of a three-million-dollar loan on the proposed office-condo complex the other side of town. Turiello had been a good client; the idea had been too seductive to walk away from. The location was ideal—a commanding precipice on the coast road, visible for miles. If the plan had worked, if the real estate market hadn't crashed, Charles, like Lidell, could have retired, and Harriet and his children would have been set. But timing (and he now knows the precise truth of this bromide) is everything. Almost immediately the market had begun to collapse, and neither he nor Turiello nor the third partner, Turiello's brother Emil, could lease or sell any of the space. At last calculation, Charles was into the bank for a million, his commission flow had trickled to almost nothing, and he now has on his desk a stack of policy lapse notices nearly half a foot high. If the bank can't sell the office soon for a decent price, Charles knows he will almost certainly lose his house as well. Already the newly compounded mortgage is crushing; his savings are nearly depleted. When he wakes in the middle of the night, the sheet below him soaked with sweat, the question he ponders is this: Will he have to put his next mortgage payment on his MasterCard?

Sometimes in the middle of the night he allows himself to think he is particularly plagued by bad luck or timing—but he has only to make this drive, as he does each day, to know he is but one of many. He can catalog the names: John Blay, Emil Turiello, Dick Lidell, Pete French . . . the list is long. Each with bombed-out fantasies, chill sweats in the night. Each scrambling now just to keep his home.

Charles rounds the last bend just before the village. Here there are Federal houses, white or pale yellow with black shutters, facing square mansions with widow's walks and larger lawns. Ship captains once built these, Charles knows, and then later sold them to the owners of the mills. Now there is only one mill owner in residence; the rest are professional offices. Two stand empty. Out in front of several there are For Sale signs. Charles's name is on some of the signs.

As a summer place, the town has always been marginal, not a town that attracts the Volvos and the Range Rovers. It is and always has been a Rhode Island fishing town, mostly Portuguese and Irish, too working-class to have supported the massive summer places farther south and west or along the coast of Connecticut. For the most part, the town has remained undiscovered, not yuppified, and Charles is glad of this, though he thinks he shouldn't be.

He passes the bank at the end of the village—The Bank—the largest building in town, an imposing stone edifice with beautifully proportioned windows and two monstrous white columns that make it look deceptively solid. It is a singular institution, a family bank, not part of a chain, the only game in town. If Charles hates passing his office, he hates having to pass this building even more, loathes particularly the fact that lately the bank is almost always on his mind. From habit, he averts his eyes, studies a knitting shop across the street.

He takes the first right at the end of the village, brings the car to rest in the driveway of his house. A hundred and forty thousand on the clock. Christ, he wonders, can the old Cadillac make it another sixty?

Charles steps out of the car, looks at the incomplete addition at the side of his house, the foundation with no building, the addition that was to have been a new kitchen for Harriet, then later an office for himself, and will now stand empty, filling up with water in a rain, and he knows it is folly to imagine oneself as the repository for all the economic troubles, that somehow it all ends with oneself. For beyond him is Antone Costa, then Costa's three sons, one of them married already, two grandchildren in eventual need of college educations. And beyond them, who? Carol Kopka, a single mother with two kids, at the checkout counter down at the A&P, the last to have been hired before the troubles? Bill Samson at the Dodge dealership, who's running thirty percent behind this year in sales? Christ, even Tom Carney at his gas station? He wonders if there is anyone in town who has escaped unscathed.

Harriet, he sees at once, has already been on the mower. The front lawn has shot up in the cooler weather, but the back lawn is trim. He could put the office in the front, he knows, where they have now a living room they hardly ever use, favoring, as they do, the family room, off the kitchen. He has been thinking about this for weeks, has reached no conclusions. He likes his house, though it is too grandiose and impractical. The house is frigid in winter, and the plumbing is mystifying—yet it's an elegant building, even if its nineteenth-century lines have begun to sag. Harriet mows the lawn, keeps the exterior tidy and painted, and minds that Charles has not solved the riddle of the plumbing—his part in this particular unspoken marital bargain.

Harriet is in the kitchen, wrestling with a large white softball of dough in a mustard-colored bowl. She has on her Sunday clothes—a pink sweatsuit and sneakers—and Charles can see that she hasn't had her shower yet: Her short, nearly black hair is still matted at one side from sleep, and there are smudges of teal blue below her lower lids. She doesn't speak as he walks in. He could tell her that he ran into Joe Medeiros, that Medeiros is pulling out of a deal, and that this will mean another stall on the addition, thus eliciting, possibly, a glance of sympathy or, at the very least, a change of subject, but as he watches her kneading the dough angrily, he decides to forgo the solicitation. More than likely, the news will simply frighten her. He puts the doughnuts on the counter, the milk in the fridge. He asks, "Where are the kids?" and she answers, not looking at him, "Outside."

He takes the newspaper into a small room off the porch that is a kind of sanctuary, a library if one were to be so formal, which he is not inclined to be. This, too, is a room that could be turned into an office, though it is a bit cramped, and he does not like having to think of giving up his retreat.

There are books in uneven stacks on the floor of the room, nearly covering the small Oriental Harriet gave him last year for Christmas. Across one of the books is a tie he wore a few days ago. A second pair of dress shoes is in a corner, and for some reason he cannot quite fathom, a pair of jeans is flung over a chair. It is another unspoken marital bargain that Harriet never enters this room, and as a consequence it is seldom cleaned, seldom tidied.

He drops the heavy Sunday paper on top of his desk, itself awash in inches of unopened mail, half-read magazines, and more books. Slipping the sweatshirt over his head, he tosses it in the direction of the chair with the jeans. On a bookshelf he has his turntable, and he puts on the Brahms Second Piano Concerto, a piece he plays often, never tires of it. It seems to him a hopeful concerto, nearly a symphony, appropriate somehow for a Sunday morning, even though the news this particular Sunday morning has not been especially hopeful. Outside, Hadley, his eldest daughter, is squealing as she takes the long, looping ride on the rope he hung for her from the tall walnut, a sail through the air that ends with a whomp in a large, forgiving pile of leaf mulch. Jack, his son, two years younger than Hadley's fourteen, is with her and is loudly demanding a turn for himself. Charles can see him through the small window of his study, squirming with impatience. He wonders briefly then where Anna, his five-year-old, is—not with them, for he would see or hear her. But he quickly dismisses the query; Harriet will know, will be watching her. For the moment he can relax.

He picks up his reading glasses from the desk, puts them on. Usually he begins with the magazine: a quick perusal of the cover story, a glance at the recipes, a longer look at the crossword to see if it's one he might tackle. This week the recipes are about blueberries—not interesting. He would study them if the dishes were Italian or Spanish or Indian. He is the cook in the family, though Harriet likes to bake, and his children often complain that what he concocts is inedible. The cover story is about the savings-and-loan scandal. He will look at that later. He picks up another thin magazine inside the paper, the weekly literary supplement.

He is thinking, as he turns the pages, of a book he has ordered at the bookstore and forgotten about; he must call to see if it is in yet. It's a volume by the French philosopher Paul Ricoeur; it must definitely be in now: he ordered it—what?—in July, he is sure. Perhaps, he is thinking as he idly peruses the table of contents, the bookstore did call, and Harriet answered and has simply forgotten to mention it to him. And it is then, in the middle of this thought, that he turns the page and sees the photograph.

His hand stops. He looks at the photograph. He lays the paper flat.

He lets his breath out slowly. He looks at the picture, reads the print around it.

It is Siân Richards. Of course he knows by the name. Another woman might conceivably have this name as well, though he thinks that unlikely. More than the name, it is her photograph that makes him certain. It is, without question, the same face, the same expression in the eyes. He brings his hand up to his face, smooths his jawline with the back of his fingers. He puts his hand down on the desk, on the newspaper, and notices that it is trembling.

He studies the photograph. The woman in the picture is now forty-five, he knows, the same age as he is. Would he know this from the photograph? He cannot say for sure. Her hair is loose, wavy; he remembers it as a kind of pale bronze, particularly in the sunlight, with glints of fresh copper wire, though it seems from the black-and-white photograph that the highlights may have become muted over time. Her face is somewhat tilted, slightly turned, so that though she looks directly at the viewer, the sense is that her face is in profile. She is not smiling, but the gaze is steady—serious yet not sad. The suggestion from the eyes is that she is poised or waiting somehow, though he cannot imagine what precisely it is that she seems to be waiting for. She is wearing large gold earrings, simple circles, and what appears to be a black sweater or soft shirt with an open neckline, like that of a ballet dancer. The photograph stops just below her breasts. He remembers her mouth.

The mouth is generous; he has not forgotten that.

He reads the print again. She is a poet. She has a book.

He holds the newspaper up—looks across the desk at the picture. He remembers the high white forehead. He cannot escape the feeling that she is looking at him.

How many years has it been? The number staggers him. He remembers with absolute clarity the first time he ever saw her. He puts the paper down, again flat on the desk. He reads the smaller print about the book of poems. He notes the publisher's name. He hears then a sound, the soft brush of fabric on wood, and he looks up to see that Harriet is in the doorway. She stands, arms crossed over her chest, resting against the jamb, observing him. Her face is not angry, but it is closed. She seems about to speak, to ask a question.

He might lift up the literary supplement and show Harriet the picture. He might say to his wife, You'll never guess who this is. Instead he does something that surprises him, that makes a faint blush of heat rise from his neck to his face and lodge behind his ears. He leans forward over the desk, arms spread, elbows cocked. With his left forearm, he shields the picture of the woman in the newspaper.

That night, when I had already entered your thoughts, I drove my husband home from the college. I had found him in a bar around the corner from the party. He'd been drinking Guinness and Bass, a string of half-and-halfs. He was sitting alone, and he tried a smile when I approached.

I said, Stephen.

He collected his change from the counter and slid off the stool. He was a gentle, brooding man, though large and muscular. He had pale blond hair, nearly white, and the high, pink color of a man who spends his days in the sun. On the right side of his face near his jaw was the shiny seam of a scar.

He let me lead him to the car and let me drive him home. He did not speak on the way, and I did not know if his silence was composed of embarrassment or bitterness or worry.

A fine dust of black dirt almost always covered the

house, despite the washings by the rain, and though the house had been painted white, it looked, from a distance, gray. The black dirt got in over the thresholds and through the cracks in the caulkings of the windows. I would find it in my drawers and on sheets that I had hung out to dry. The black dirt was nourishing and fertile, the richest soil in the state, but it seeped in everywhere, blew across the floor, coated sills and mantels. I sometimes scrubbed the woodwork until the paint wore through.

I went upstairs to see my daughter. I opened the door to Lily's room, peeked in to see the tiny body in its bed.

Then there was my study, Stephen's office, the bedroom that we shared. Stephen went into his office and shut the door.

When I had paid the baby-sitter and taken her home, I went back into the house and sat at the kitchen table. I had made an effort to give the room warmth, and there was a vase of mauve and brown hydrangeas on the pine table. I took off the jacket I had worn over my dress and laid it along the back of a chair. I took off my shoes, undid the pins from my hair. I sat down.

It was raining, a light drizzle that had come with the afternoon clouds, and on the windows the droplets lit up in the headlights of a car. Beyond the front yard, I could hear that particular sound of tires on a gravel road.

I thought then that I should go to Stephen. There are always, in any partnership, balances and debts and payments. But I know I hoped instead that he had fallen asleep on the couch in his office. He often slept there.

Perhaps, as I sat at the kitchen table, I replayed certain phrases from the party. Perhaps I thought about the morning, about a class I had to prepare for. Possibly I did actually wonder if anyone from my past would see the advertisement in the Sunday paper. Or did I merely peer into the vase, a polished ceramic surface that gave off a rose sheen like a mirror, and study the distorted image of my face?

When visitors came over the mountain and first saw the valley, the dirt was so astonishingly black and the landscape so unrelievedly flat that the visitors thought what they saw was tar. And sometimes they said that: A parking lot? A landing field?

I often wonder now; What would have happened if that first letter had not been sent on to me, if it had lain unattended in a folder or on a desk? Or if it had been lost?

I have your shirt still, but the scent is fading.

HE HAS BEEN BACK IN HIS STUDY NOW FOR TWENTY MIN-
utes, and he cannot find anything suitable. Outside, a
cloud bank from the west has begun to cover the sun,
letting through only a thin wash of light. His children
are in the house somewhere: Hadley, he thinks, is upstairs, finishing her homework; he is not sure where
Jack and Anna are. He can still taste the roast from
Harriet's mother's, a leg of lamb that was, inevitably,
too well done. No one in Harriet's family can cook, he
has long decided, and the table invariably looks
stingy—even on Thanksgiving. He had forgotten that
they were expected at his in-laws' until Harriet had
come to the door of his study to remind him. He was
distracted at dinner, focused on a face.

He has the paper folded to the ad and has arranged
it so that it looks casually tossed upon his desk. He has
found a box of Audubon bird cards, is not sure that
they will do. Harriet, he knows, may have stationery,

but he certainly cannot ask her. In any event, it's un-likely to be appropriate for the occasion; he has an idea that her writing paper will be the color of cotton candy and will have scrollwork down the sides. He sifts through the papers in his top left-hand drawer. There's a Hopper print, but it's of a middle-aged couple in front of a house, and they don't look particularly happy. Does he have nothing plain and simple? He pulls out a thin sheet of blue airmail stationery, looks at his watch. Five past four. What's open?

He puts on the hooded sweatshirt, checks his back pocket to make sure he has his wallet. He slides the keys from the kitchen counter, snaps the screen door shut. Harriet is raking along the ell, already removing the first leaves of the season. She has her back to him. He watches as she bends and pulls. She has on jeans, an aqua sweater. The tines of the rake scrape along the dirt, obscure the sound of his leaving. She doesn't turn around. He hesitates, observing her.

He loves her more than he used to, he does know that. He does not like to think about the early years of their marriage, when he would sometimes wake in the night, his heart racing, stricken with the knowledge that he and she had both made a terrible mistake. That fear, foundering and bobbing in the early mornings like a stick tossed upon a chop, would make him irritable, and they often fought. He remembers the fights—shrill words he thought could never be taken back. But then Harriet had become pregnant with Hadley, and their life together—the pregnancies, the babies, the house, the building of his business—had become a project that made them quieter, easier together, and he no longer allowed himself to ponder the question of whether or not he had made a mistake. How could he regret the decisions he had made that led to Hadley and to Jack and to Anna? It was to him almost a physical impossibility, like juggling, which he has attempted several times to impress his children but has never mastered.

He watches her stoop to remove a rock. Her jeans are tight along the backs of her thighs. Since Anna she has not lost the extra ten pounds she has wanted to lose, despite her vigorous and sometimes comical early morning walks with the hand weights. He has tried to tell her that she looks fine as she is, which is true but does not explain why they seldom make love anymore. He does not understand it himself exactly, except that it is harder now to get through the day without the small irritations that lead to resignation.

He knows, too, that it is not Harriet who often demurs in the bedroom at night, but rather himself. Always, his wife asked for and accepted their sexual life as a given—even in those early years, when there was little love between them. For that he might be grateful, though he often feels that while she is essentially present in the bed, perhaps even in the entire marriage itself, he somehow is not.

The fan rake catches on a rock, bends the tine. He thinks of calling to her, taking the rake, straightening the tine for her, but he stops himself, watches instead as she ignores the rake's bent finger and drags the tool even more aggressively across the ground.

They are not alike, he and Harriet, a fact that he knows was a source of his tension in the early years of their marriage. A tension that has become a mild discomfort whenever he has to be alone with her. They do not talk much together, and he knows that despite the children and the house, they have little in common. It is not just the obvious dissimilarities—that he is an Irish Catholic and she a Yankee Congregationalist, despite the fact they virtually never attend church (nor do the children); or that he grew up in working-class Providence while she spent her childhood in the suburbs; or even that he cannot quite escape the old thought patterns of sin and redemption, while she seems never to have imagined a life in terms of transgressions and payments. No, it is instead, he thinks, the smaller truths, the almost inconsequential ones, that carry with them the greater weight: That she has plans for any given day and seldom deviates from them, is almost never late, and at the end of the day can add up the experiences, the completed tasks, and find among them some satisfaction, while he squanders time, resists the effort necessary to complete a task, thinks of his drives to the beach as the highlights of his day. Or the small truth that she has never once, in their entire marriage, played a piece of music for herself, never put a cassette into the tape recorder, never put a record on the turntable, and that when she drives she prefers silence to the radio. Or the small fact (although perhaps, he thinks, this ought to be a larger fact) that she believes wholeheartedly in the ritual of the family dinner at six, even though his stomach almost always seizes up at that hour and doesn't begin to relax until later in the evening. Many nights he stands at the kitchen counter at nine o'clock and eats alone a dish that he has made, and if she walks through the kitchen then, she almost always asks him what he's doing there.

Sometimes this information—the small truths and the larger ones—puzzles him: how one can be with a woman for so many years, ostensibly have shared so many intimacies (how many times have they made love, he wonders—two thousand? three thousand?), and yet still feel fundamentally unknown in her presence.

She did not hear him leave the house, but she will hear the car starting, so he calls to her.

"Harriet."

She turns to face him. Her hair is fixed in place, and she has on her makeup.

"Where are you going?" she asks.

"Out," he says. "An errand."

"What errand?" She frowns slightly, a reflexive gesture more than a comment. Her hand is poised on the top of the rake.

His mind flails and leaps. What errand on a Sunday afternoon?

"Tires," he says.

"Tires?"

"I'm worried about the tread. Thought I'd get them checked out. Before the weather turns."

"Oh." She looks puzzled.

Charles flings open the door of the car, puts the key in the ignition. Although he does not look at her again, he knows his wife is studying him as he backs the Cadillac out of the drive.

Costa's Card & Gift is just past the pharmacy. He flips his blinker on to pull into a space in front of the store, then abruptly turns it off. Jesus Christ, he can't go in there. Janet Costa, Antone's wife, is a class mother with Harriet, and Janet owns and manages the store. He can hear the dialogue: Saw Charles on Sunday in the store. Charles? He was buying stationery. Stationery? What kind of stationery?

He will have to drive to the mall. The bookstore there sells note cards and writing paper. He checks his watch again. It's a twenty-minute ride. The mall should still be open.

The route to the mall takes him along 59, a county highway so densely packed with fast-food restaurants and discount stores that it looks more like Florida than the coast of New England. Yet even here the recession has claimed its victims: an appliance center is boarded up; the windows of a ski shop are empty, the fake snow still cascading across the glass. He thinks briefly of Joe Medeiros, pushes the thought from his mind.

The bookstore is small and appealing—surprisingly so for a shop located in a mall. There is, when he enters, an abundance of wood and Essex green, a wicker rocking chair by a pot of coffee, books with glossy jackets arranged on tables and shelves. Along one wall, he sees several stands of note cards. He heads in that direction.

He turns the wire stands slowly, looks at the rows of

cards. A young woman in a black sweater asks him if he needs help.

"I need paper," he says, looking at the woman. "Writing paper. Simple. Heavy."

The woman bends to retrieve a box in a cabinet beneath a counter.

"I don't have paper," she says, "but I have these."

He takes the box from her and opens it. Inside are stiff heavy cards, about the size of wedding invitations. Below them are envelopes that match. The color is ivory.

"They're our best," she says.

"This will do," he says, "and I need a good pen, if you sell them. A fountain pen."

This last request has occurred to Charles only as he has uttered it. He will have to write the note in the car. He cannot write it at home.

They walk together to the register. Charles hands the woman a credit card, wonders fleetingly if he's already over the limit—a staggering amount of money in itself. "Wait a minute," he says. "I have a book on order here. And I need another book too, although I don't know if you have it."

He tells the saleswoman the names of the books. He adds that the second is a book of poetry. She checks in the computer, says that his order came in and that they have five of the volumes of poetry—the shipment arrived last week.

"I'll get it for you," she says.

When she hands the small book to him, Charles studies the jacket, turns the book over. The photograph he saw in the advertisement is on the back. He reads the short biography that accompanies the picture: "This is Siân Richards' third collection of poetry. She lives in eastern Pennsylvania with her husband and daughter."

This last sentence seems impossible to him—as if he had been told that the earth had four moons. Or that the tides had stopped.

The bridge is desolate, empty at five-twenty on a Sunday. He parks on the blacktop at its end. The cloud cover is thick now, a grayish-brown batting, darker behind him in the west. Soon there will be splashes on the windshield. The temperature has changed too; it's dropped ten, fifteen degrees since noon, he thinks. Beside him is the book of poems, the box of stationery, the pen. He picks up the book, rests it against the steering wheel, turns each page slowly. He reaches down in front of the passenger seat, fumbles for a beer in the cooler. Still cold; the label is wet.

He reads each of the poems, then closes the book. He makes a desk with it on his lap, resting one edge on the steering wheel. He unscrews the pen, slips in a cartridge, makes a few practice scrawls on the paper bag from the bookstore. The rain begins, tentatively at first, a slow, uneven rain of fat drops. He likes the sound of the rain on the roof of his car, the isolation of the beach. He takes a card from the box, lays it on the book. He puts the pen to the card.

He cannot think how to begin. He takes a long swallow of beer, then hears a phrase, a single phrase of a song. Jesus Christ. He turns the book over to look again at the picture. The phrase comes to him again, blown off across the sand. He plays it in his mind, and then again, even as he played the 45 over and over as a boy.

Fragments rush in upon him now. A young girl's face. A high white forehead. A blue dress just below the knees. A stone courtyard.

Images and ideas scud along the crust of sand in front of him, pockmarked now with the beginning of the rain.

The song may be on a jukebox somewhere, he thinks. He cannot remember all the words, just the tune, bits of phrases. He looks down at the thick white card on the book.

He thinks: I cannot do this. I have a wife and three children, and I may lose the house soon.

Then he thinks: How can I not do this?

"Dear Siân," he writes.

*** *** *** *** *** *** *** *** *** *Two*

Dear Siân,

When I saw your picture in this morning's
newspaper I had the same feeling as I had the
first time I saw you, in the courtyard of The Ridge
thirty-one years ago. I bought your new book of poetry
today. I have read all the poems once, and will
need to spend more time with them, but I was
struck initially by the way the bleak emotional and
physical landscape you describe takes on a unique
beauty. Beauty out of deprivation. And how this
theme holds true as well in the several poems
about the migrant workers. I hope you have not had
to experience what you write about.

Congratulations.

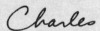

Dear Charles,

I was delighted to get your note. Can it really
have been thirty-one years ago? I have an image
of the boy you were then—and somewhere I have
photographs of you, even one, I think, of the two of
us. Weren't you called Cal, or did I dream that?

I live on a farm with my husband and my
daughter, Lily, who is three. Two days a week, I teach
poetry at Stryker University, not far from my home.

*Thank you for your comments about the poems. The
landscape I write about is familiar to me. As are
the migrant workers.*

*You know what I do and what I look like. I am more
than a little curious about what you do and what you
look like.*

——————————————————————— September 26

Dear Siân,

Somewhere my children still have a gold
identity card hanging from a chain, with "Cal"
written on the front and "Siân" written by you on
the back.

I am married, with three beautiful children—
fourteen, twelve, and five.

I am surprised your daughter is so young. I suppose
I just assumed you had married earlier and that your
child would be nearly grown.

I plotted the bike ride between my house and
yours several times, but a 200-mile bike ride across
three states is pretty difficult for a fourteen-year-old
boy. Did your father ever tell you that I called
about a year after we had each graduated from
college?

Concerning what I do, I sell both insurance and
real estate. I'm doing brilliantly at neither at the
moment.

To know what I look like, you'll have to meet me for a drink.

Thank you for not making me write to you through your publisher. That would be tiresome.

Charles

———————————————— October 15

Dear Siân,

I am just a little concerned that you have not responded to my last letter. I hope this correspondence has not put you off in some way.

I remember I saw you as soon as I arrived at The Ridge. I can picture this vividly. You were standing in the courtyard, in a cotton dress with short sleeves, and it came down below your knees. It must have been just after we had arrived. I remember, too, the first time we spoke to each other.

We were painfully shy with one another. I do remember that. I remember walking down to the lake in an agony as to whether or not I would have the courage to hold your hand. I believe I also gave you a gold bracelet that said "The Ridge" on it. I remember the badminton game. And, of course, I have never forgotten the bonfire. Do you remember that?

I find it extraordinary that I should have the same feeling looking at your picture in the advertisement

that I had thirty-one years ago looking at a
beautiful young girl in a courtyard.

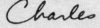

———————————————————————————— October 20

Dear Charles,
  No, I have not been put off by this
correspondence, though I am unclear as to just
where it is going. But perhaps I am being too linear.
It doesn't have to go anywhere, I suppose; it might
just circle and loop around in our memories.
  I am fascinated by your memories. I would love
sometime to compare them—yours and mine. Did you
perceive that week as I did, I wonder? I do see myself
with you. I am wearing a white sleeveless blouse
and plaid pedal pushers, and my hair is pulled back
in a ponytail. You are beside me, quite a bit taller,
and you have a crew cut. I must have this image from
a photograph. I will go through my trunk and find
all of the photographs one day soon.
  I do remember the bracelet and the badminton game
and the night of the bonfire. I also remember having
an epiphany of sorts, down by the outdoor chapel
at the water's edge, that the essence of religion was
love, pure and simple. I am not religious now, by the
way. I haven't been inside a church, except for a wedding
or a funeral, in twenty years.
  I would, of course, meet you for a drink, but I

*think you will be disappointed. I am not quite as
interesting or as mysterious as my photograph makes
me out to be.*

—————————————————————————————— October 23

Dear Siân,

I received your letter yesterday. I saw the
review of your new book in last Sunday's literary
supplement. I was thrilled when I saw it, and I
thought it was quite good, all in all. I know it must
be hard to have your work hanging out there
for anyone to take aim at. I confess I seldom
read poetry—at least contemporary poetry: I am
more likely to read philosophy or history—so I was
a little lost and befuddled in the paragraph of
comparisons to other poets, but I felt the
reviewer was absolutely right when he referred to
you as a transcendentalist.

I can remember being with you at the outdoor
chapel by the water. If the essence of religion
is love, and you love someone as I'm sure you do,
then I guess you're religious. Those are words from
a former seminarian. After college I entered the
seminary and was there for two years. Mostly I
wanted to avoid the draft, but I probably received
my best education there. I haven't been to church
in twenty years either.

There is a line in a book I read recently about
the curiosity of lives unfolding. I guess that is
what we are doing. I know you are interesting.
The part of you that I believe is mysterious we could
hold on to by not meeting, but I wouldn't be satisfied
with just holding on to a mystery.

Just tell me where and when. Whatever is
easiest for you. I'm looking forward to meeting you.
Again.

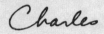

—————————————————————————— *October 28*

Dear Charles,
*I would like to meet with you sometime, although
I confess I am a bit uneasy. My larger difficulty,
however, is that I feel uncomfortable in the position
of having to arrange a meeting. I don't know quite
what else to say at this point, except that I will
think about it. I don't mean to put you off, but
I am a little daunted by the hows and wheres.*

*I'm sorry you had to see the review in the literary
supplement. It is probably a classic example of a
"mixed" review, but it stung nevertheless.*

*I smiled at the image of your plotting the bike ride
from your house to mine. My father still lives in the
same house in which I grew up in Springfield, but
I really left western Massachusetts when I went to
college. I attended a Catholic college for women in*

*New Hampshire and barely escaped entering religious
orders myself by joining the Peace Corps. My mother
died while I was in college. In the Peace Corps, I taught
elementary school in Senegal. When I returned to
this country, I went to graduate school for a time,
and I met my husband there. Then we settled on his
farm.*

*What is it like where you live, and what are the
names of your children?*

*I am sorry my handwriting is so poor. I could type
these letters if you'd rather—your handwriting is
remarkably beautiful.*

*I am intrigued by how you happen to have a
postbox.*

Siân

————————————————————————— November 1

Dear Siân,

  I had already ordered from my local bookstore
your two previous books, and several days ago
your first book of poetry, about Africa, arrived. I think
the poems are beautiful—that goes without saying.
There are threads and currents that run through
your poetry, but each poem is somehow a
surprise. I'd also like to say, and I hope this is not
disturbing to you, that I think there is a kind of sadness
associated with your poetry. This is easier to see

in the later poems—a kind of awful loneliness,
I think. Or do I only imagine that?

I'd like to see you smile. You seem fairly
serious, and I'm sorry about the "sting" of the
review.

I knew that your mother had died. Your father
told me when I spoke to him on the telephone.

Our lives seem to have been running on parallel
tracks. I mean by that only the coincidences of having
small children, of both having entered or nearly
entered religious orders, and of both having
lapsed. Perhaps when we meet, we will discover other
similarities.

I live in a middle-to-working-class coastal
fishing village, in a large white house badly in
need of repair. Unfortunately I'm fairly lazy, so it
will probably stay in need of repair.

I went to Holy Cross, then to seminary in
Chicago. After that I drove a city bus. I was
driving the city bus when my sister's husband was
killed in a car accident, and I had to come home
to help her take over her husband's business.
Then she remarried and went off to Los Angeles,
and I got stuck with the business. The rest, as they
say, is history.

The town I live in is about a half hour from
Providence, where I was living when we met as
children.

My children are Hadley, fourteen; Jack, twelve;
and Anna, five. I think each is beautiful and
unique.

When I first wrote you, I thought we could have a casual meeting. Now every letter I write you, I feel I risk scaring you away. Putting the burden of the "where and when" of our meeting on you was really just the concern of someone who knows what it's like to have a three-year-old child. I can set up the time and place and arrange for a chaperone.

I'd rather write you in longhand, and thanks for the compliment about my handwriting, but I had to get this out in a hurry. The only reason I have a P.O. box is that I run my business out of it, and I can get the mail earlier.

It takes time to read between the lines.

I notice that you don't say much about your husband.

Charles

———————————————————— November 5

Dear Charles,

I am leaving for Cambridge, England, on Thursday and will be away teaching a poetry seminar for two weeks. I wanted to say, before I left, that I like the letters you write to me, that I like the things you choose to say.

Yes, I am often too serious, and no, you are not wrong if you sometimes see sadness in my work. These are characteristics I don't seem to be able to do much about.

Thank you, but I won't need a chaperone.
I notice that you say little about your wife.

Siân

November 7

Dear Siân,

Touché.

Going to England is one hell of a good excuse for not being able to meet with me. For whom are you teaching? Do you do this sort of thing often?

I am disappointed. If I knew what flight you were taking, I'd drive to the airport and see you off, though that would be incredibly frustrating.

Please send me a postcard from England. I probably won't get it before you're home, but do it anyway.

I miss you already.

Charles

November 10

Dear Charles,

My plane is leaving in a few hours, but I had to send these pictures off to you before I left. For some reason I cannot explain, I was seized this afternoon with a desire to go through my trunks and find the photographs I thought were there. I am sending

*you these two—the one of us together in the
courtyard and the shot of the lake taken from the
outdoor chapel. I'm sure that the one of us was
taken on the last day, just before we had to leave. How
extraordinary what the memory got right and what
it didn't. You look much as I had remembered you
(do you still have somewhere that wonderful old
Brownie that is in your hand?). But I look very different.
I didn't remember the Bermuda shorts or that my hair
was quite that light ever. Nor that you and I were
the same height. Your arm is around me, but just
barely, and I'm unable at all to meet the gaze of the
camera. I seem to be studying my feet.*

*Aren't the photographs concrete proof that
somewhere in time we did actually meet and know
each other? What did we know? I wonder. And what
did our voices sound like?*

*This archaeological dig has consumed nearly all
my afternoon, and I'm not even packed yet. I must
run, but I wanted you to have this. One day I will
find the bracelet. I'm sure I must have it. I never throw
anything away.*

I promise a postcard.

_____ November 15

Dear Siân,
    I drove to the beach today to look out toward

Portugal, but there was a haze on the water, and the view was obscured.

Actually, I often go to the beach and look out toward Portugal. This activity consumes more of my time than it ought to.

This letter is hard to write, knowing you are far away and won't even read it for at least a week. I wonder what it is like for you in England, what you are doing. I imagine you with a long scarf wrapped around your neck, walking along a path toward a beautiful stone building where your students are waiting for you.

I was moved by your archaeological dig and by the two photographs. It was the last day of camp, and we had asked someone to take the picture of us together. I remember that my parents had arrived already, before yours, and that they were standing off at some distance, watching us, barely masking their impatience. I also remember that I cried all the way home in the car and that when I told my mother I had given you a gold bracelet with the words "The Ridge" on it, she said to me: "So where's *my* bracelet?"

What happened to me thirty-one years ago was love at first sight. I don't understand the phenomenon entirely, and I'm more than a little embarrassed at having to resort to the clichés of old 45s, but I can remember vividly that gut-wrenching feeling. I am less clear about what happened to me when I saw your picture in the newspaper two months ago. Last night I was reading Paul Ricoeur, and a line of his stopped me: "the fulfillment of an antecedent meaning which remained in suspense." He meant the irrational irruption of Jesus Christ in the context of the New Testament, but I tend to take bits where I find them and apply them to my own life. The difficulty for me is that I can't completely absorb what happened thirty-one years ago or on September 15, because I don't have enough access to the antecedent.

All this means is that I want to meet the woman who has grown from the girl I remember.

Time has taken on a new dimension. I feel the chaos of time, but I'm trying to comprehend it in relationship to loss. I spent all of August with Stephen Hawking, thinking about "quarks" and black holes, but he didn't mention how waiting for a letter or recrossing a warp of thirty-one years to a young girl's face can make time fold in upon itself. My daughter is now the same age as we were then, a "fact" of physics or of nature that baffles me.

Perhaps I am looking only for an open connection.

Today has more warmth than you would imagine for the fifteenth of November. The ocean was a dusty blue when I drove to the beach earlier, with the haze on the horizon. There was a stillness this afternoon, both visual and sensual, that was soporific—or at least that's the excuse I am using to explain why I dozed for twenty minutes in my car with the sun warming the front seat through

the windshield. At the beach, across a long wooden
bridge from the mainland, you can hear the bells
from the church tower in the center of town, and
I like listening to them, interspersed with the
calling of the gulls. Even the gulls were half
asleep today, though—enjoying this short Indian-
summer respite from a string of cold gray days. I
nearly missed my lunch appointment.

You mention my wife, and I mention your
husband, and we receive in reply only further questions
or silences. I might one day be able to speak to you
or write you about my marriage, but I am more
engaged now (and have been for some time) with
the sound of bells from a church tower or the
mysterious physics of time. What to reveal and what
to conceal is perplexing to me.

For the same reason that I cannot focus on
my marriage, my business is shot to hell. I used
to be better at compartmentalizing. I'm supposed
to sell insurance and real estate, but the entire
town is under siege, and every dime is frozen.
I could write you more about this, but I'd like to
keep the shit out of this correspondence. I'd like
to transcend the shit, is what I'd like to do.
Actually, I do not always hate my job. I used
to like to talk to people about what was important
to them.

Where does the pain in your poetry come
from?

I imagine going to a market in Cambridge and

buying ingredients for a meal that I would make
for you. I love to cook. Am I going too far?

Yesterday I called The Ridge to see if it was still
there. You will probably not be surprised to learn
that it has been turned into an inn. I asked the
woman who answered the phone if she had a brochure
with a photograph so that I could see what it looked
like now. She said the only exterior shot was the
building itself with the fountain. Did I remember
the fountain? I said yes, but that my most vivid memory
was of the girl I met there thirty-one years ago. She
said: "Did you marry her?" I said: "No, but I
should have."

Now I *know* I am going too far.

Sometimes I think we are both too serious. If you
want me to stop, just tell me. I know this can
end in an instant.

I know we have to meet. I think you know that
as well.

I could tell you so much more, but I really just
want to hold your hand.

As I sit here trying to compose a letter that will
mean something to you, I can't take my eyes off
your picture. You said in a letter that you are not
interesting and not mysterious, but you didn't say
that you are not beautiful.

Charles

———————————————— *November 16, London*

Dear Charles,

  *Today I took a walk in Regent's Park. I'd love
to see it in the summer when the roses are in bloom.
I'm in London for talks with my British publisher.
They've put me up at a wonderful hotel on the Strand.
Downstairs in the pub, they serve forty different
kinds of malt whiskey. Last night I tried three and
was nearly paralyzed. Today is my birthday.*

  Cheers,

  Siân

———————————————— *November 28*

Dear Charles,

  I want this to stop. I'm sorry.

  *It has been a very long time since anyone wanted
to, or wanted only to, hold my hand.*

  *I do not know you, but I sometimes think I have
felt who you are in your letters.*

  Siân

———————————————— *November 30*

Dear Siân,

  Regarding your last letter, there is a wonderful
story about Jack and Bobby Kennedy during the

Cuban missile crisis. You probably already know it,
but I'm going to tell it to you anyway. Reducing
it to its essentials, the story goes like this. At a crucial
moment in the negotiations, Jack Kennedy gets a
telegram from Khrushchev that's fairly
conciliatory and suggests that Khrushchev is
going to back off. Just as Jack and Bobby are about
to celebrate, however, Khrushchev fires off another
telegram. This one is hostile and essentially tells
Kennedy that he's changed his mind about
backing off. What to do? Bobby has a brilliant idea.
Ignore the second telegram, pretend they never got
it, and immediately go on national TV, thanking
Khrushchev for his humane gesture—thus ending
the crisis.

   Your comment about holding your hand will haunt
me forever.

   The enclosed device has many possibilities, but
I hope you'll use it to listen to the tape I am sending
with it. Sorry for the sound quality, but some of these
songs are as old as I am. A number of them had
to come off a jukebox.

   I know you could order a similar tape with an
800 number and your credit card, but it wouldn't
be the same. I tried for the time that might
bring us back together, if only for a moment.
My favorite song is "Where or When." The B side
of that record, "That's My Desire," is a close second.
This may mean nothing to you. There is a gap
on one side where I screwed up. Just be patient.
If you can't be that, just put it in the trash compactor.

We have a reservation for lunch at The Ridge for next Thursday at twelve noon. I'm including with this letter directions from your house.

I thought it unfair to meet for lunch and not allow you to know what I look like when I know what you look like, so I am sending along this picture. It isn't very good, but I don't have many. My daughter took it last summer when she and I were fishing. The fish is a striped bass. On Thursday at noon I won't be holding the fish, and I hope I won't be left holding the bag.

Charles

ssssssss *Three*

$\mathscr{I}$was working in my office when I heard the familiar sound of the engine of the mailman's jeep, the squeak of the mailbox being opened, the firm slap of metal upon metal. It was a signal, as it almost always was, to leave my desk, as if I had been summoned by the outside world. Lily was at the house where she was watched during the mornings by a neighbor. Stephen was in the barn, working on the cultivator.

It was chilly as I walked out front to get the mail, and I was thinking that when I went back inside, I would make myself another cup of coffee. Inside the mailbox, there was a large envelope from my publisher, and inside that a smaller envelope with my name on it. I took all the mail inside.

The envelope with my name on it was the color of thick cream; the ink was a dark navy. My name had been written in a beautiful hand, strong and large and steady. Simple, not pretentious. I thought: This must be an invitation. I remember I ran my finger across the ink of my name, as though it might have texture.

And when I read the letter, I thought: *Cal.*

I saw a boy, a tall boy with soft brown eyes and a crew cut—and for weeks, even after we had met, when I thought of you I would see this boy.

I could see the lake with the wooden benches, a wooden cross, not ornate. I could see the length of you, the span of you from your waist to your shoulders, in your arms and in your legs. In those days, boys wore white shirts and black pants, even in the summer.

I could see the woods, a patch of woods, in the moonlight.

I went upstairs and put the letter in a drawer, under other papers, where it could not be seen.

I made my husband's lunch and called to him. I put on my jacket and walked to my neighbor's house, where I picked up my daughter. My life went on as usual. I put dishes in the dishwasher, held my small girl, ran my fingers through her fine blond hair. Stephen came and went, and there were long silences between us. There was a kind of tightness around his eyes, which was new to me. He had migraines—two, I think—from the time your letter came until I answered it.

Some nights, after dinner, Stephen and I would talk about the farm, replaying worn scenarios. There was my father, but we had borrowed from him already, and he had almost nothing left. There were more acres we might sell if we could find a buyer. It was the second year of a failed crop, an insupportable burden. Stephen had taken on another job, as a part-time instructor at the agricultural school.

After we had talked, however briefly, Stephen would go up to his office and shut the door. Often I would find him there in the mornings, asleep in his jeans and a sweater.

I didn't mind sleeping alone; in fact, I believe I welcomed it. But sometimes, waking in the middle of the night and walking down the darkened hallway to look in on Lily, I would have a hollow sensation within me, a certainty that I had failed with Stephen, a fear that my life would be defined by this missed connection. Stephen had needed me to fill his emptiness, to assuage the intensity of the black dirt and of his ties to the farm, but I hadn't been able to do that for him.

Stephen had always been secretive—a gentle man, but a hard man to know. Once when I'd asked him about the scar, that shiny seam on his jaw, he said he'd had an accident with a gun some years before I met him and that a bullet had grazed his chin. But when he told this fact to me, he averted his eyes, and I saw something in his face more revealing than the telltale scar. And always, after that, I was watchful.

Had I really ever loved my husband? I think I must have in the beginning, drawn as I had been to his reserve, his anomalous grace, and what I thought, mistaking silence for self-containment, was an appealing dignity. But love, I now know, is an imprecise word, a relative term. I believe you loved your wife, in your way. I believe Stephen thought he loved me.

I waited for the second letter and the third. I learned

to listen more keenly for the sound of the mailman's jeep, and I began to anticipate the cream envelopes with the navy-blue ink. I tried to imagine who you were and what you looked like as a grown man, but I could not think beyond the tall, thin boy with the crew cut. I would take the letters you had sent and reread them in my office, trying to extrapolate from the boy, trying to feel who you might be. I wondered what you could remember and how it was you had developed such a clear hand. And in the mornings, before waking, I began to dream of you.

On the day I left for England, I was thinking about meeting you again after all those years. It was late, and I had not finished packing, and I new that I should concentrate on that activity. Stephen was at the college. I had clothes out on the bed—sweaters and skirts, stockings and a robe. I looked at them and thought: I have to find the picture.

The attic was a cramped crawl space, an alcove into which I tossed things from time to time—the Christmas box, winter quilts, summer quilts—and tidied once a year. I could not stand up in the attic and so made my way, bent over from the waist, to the place where I had stored my trunk. It was a large, heavy wooden trunk that had traveled from Springfield to Dakar and back to this country and to the attic of this farm. In it were letters from my grandmother, scented letters on lavender stationery written in a small hand with purple ink. I had saved the corsages from high school dances, flat brown mementos in waxed paper, with the names of boys attached. There were diaries, ribboned piles of more letters, African sculptures in black wood, a grade school picture in a gold frame, a piece of cloth from Senegal I'd forgotten about, an oval photograph of my mother as a young girl that I took out and dusted off and thought resembled Lily and how I would put it on the piano in the living room for her to see.

Then, at the bottom of the trunk, there was the album of photographs, an album I had put together when I was fourteen. In it were three photographs from the week we had together, and I kept one. You and I are standing in front of the fountain, and again you have your arm around me. But the photographer (who was it, I wonder now—a girlfriend of mine? my mother? a counselor?) has caught us in the act of laughing or of moving apart, and our bodies and our faces are turned away from each other. Your arm is still on my back, and in the picture my eyes are closed, and I am smiling.

When I returned from England and saw the letter waiting for me, I became afraid. Stephen had put it on my desk, unopened. I did not think he would ever open a letter addressed to me, but I could not be certain. Already the correspondence would have been impossible to explain: Why was I writing to you at all?

I wrote you that I wanted it to stop, but I know I hoped you wouldn't hear me.

The package with the tape recorder and the headphones was sitting atop the mailbox, and I thought when I saw it that it must be visible for a hundred miles, even through the thick planking of the barn. I held it cradled in my arm as I walked into the house, thinking: I don't want this, I don't want him to send me gifts.

The photograph alarmed me. You didn't look at all like the boy I had been imagining. Your face was turned to the side. I couldn't see your eyes. You were wearing a windbreaker, and your hair was blowing from what seemed to be a stiff breeze. I could see that you were tall, or possibly, I thought, that was only the angle of the camera. Behind you there was a lighthouse and a cliff.

I hid the tape recorder and the headphones in the drawer with the letters. I went downstairs to make Lily's lunch. I put on my jacket to walk to my neighbor's house to get my daughter.

All the farms backed onto the dirt as onto water—a vast, inky sea. Some houses were not five feet from the black dirt; it seemed to run straight to the foundations, a dark flood. I was still often surprised by the colors of the houses—pink and aqua and mint green—and I thought they must have been painted that way to dispel the monochrome of the landscape. Behind most of the farmhouses there were metal barns in brittle pastels, and in the yards there was often wash on the line. It was a fine day, sharp and clear and cold.

Almost all of the farmers now were Polish. The Rutkowski farm; the Bogdanski farm; the Sieczek farm; the Krysch farm. St. Stanislaus was the center of the town. When I met Stephen, I had thought the life of farming romantic. I did not know how hard it was— how lonely.

The walk to my neighbor's house took only minutes.

By many of the farms there were onion crates stacked like lobster pots. I liked the piles of onions at the edge of the black fields behind the houses; the piles were red and rust and a shiny, tawny yellow in the sunlight. At harvest, the eyes stung for days.

The farms had little privacy. They were exposed to the black plains, a geological accident. I passed an old graveyard with Dutch names, and beyond that a wooden barn in disrepair. Out of sight over the hill was migrant-worker housing—long, low, flat buildings, two windows and a door to each unit, gray cement blocks. Out in front of this housing was a rusted swing set the children never used.

I could not leave the town or Stephen. We had had a boy early, and after he was gone, I didn't think of leaving. Our son was buried in the Polish cemetery behind St. Stanislaus, where we had been married.

Lily was waiting for me with her jacket on, her nose pressed against the glass of the front door. We made the journey back to the house slowly. Lily played as we walked, picked up stones and bottle caps, treasures to save in the pockets of her jacket. She had soft, pale hair from her father, which I liked to feel with my fingers.

I put Lily to bed for a nap and went downstairs to begin the laundry. Stephen was sitting at the kitchen table, in early from the work in the barn. He wore his jacket still, was rubbing his forehead as if there might be another headache coming. I asked him if he wanted lunch. He shook his head no. I sat down, waited.

I saw a package, he said, on the mailbox. I meant to bring it in to you. Did you get it?

I said yes.

What was it? he asked.

Extra books, I said. I looked away.

He said, Oh.

I decided then that I would reseal the package and send it back to you. I thought that I would tell you again that this would have to stop. I tried to tell myself that the consequences might be severe, that already I had committed a kind of betrayal that would not be understood. But I did not reseal the package, and it remained hidden in my desk for days, untouched and unreturned.

On the night before you had asked me to meet you, Stephen was called away to a meeting at the college. I had put Lily to bed. I took the tape recorder and the headphones from the desk drawer and walked with them into the bedroom. It was a small room, in which a double bed was dominant. I had made a quilt, a white quilt with patches of rose and green, to give the room color and light, but it was always dark even so. There was just the one window, which looked out over the black dirt and on the glass there were rivulets of a fine dust that had been disturbed by the rain.

I can tell you about the bedroom. It doesn't matter now.

I had a glass of wine with me that I had poured after supper. I lay down on the bed, did not turn on the lights. I fumbled with the machine in the dark, plugged the headphones in, put them on. I had never listened to music with headphones before, had never experienced the way the music seems to be inside the brain.

I played the first song, and I smiled. It reminded me of CYO dances as a girl; of dark gymnasiums with loud, slow dreamy music; of awkward embraces with boys who were often shorter than myself then. Of my face sometimes muffled into a taller boy's shoulder.

I played the second song and sat up in bed. I laughed. I thought: This is a kind of excavation.

I played the third song, and the memories flooded in upon me. A kiss at the nape of the neck. A butterfly.

I played the fourth song, and I began to cry.

🌿 🌿 🌿 🌿 🌿 🌿

HE WAKES FOR THE FIFTH TIME AND CAN SEE, TO HIS RE-
lief, by the faint suggestion of light at the edges of the
shade at the window, that it is finally early morning. He
stirs slightly, not wanting to disturb Harriet, but something in his movements, the slight tug of the sheet perhaps, makes her turn toward him, murmuring in her
half sleep. He feels then her fingers, her hand reaching
for him, the practiced, sleepy gesture meant to mas-
sage, to bring him along. He sucks his stomach in,
shifts slightly so that he is just beyond her reach, hoping that she is not yet quite conscious enough to notice
this gentle rebuff. Not this morning.

He studies his wife in the gray light of predawn. She
seems to be burrowing, lying on her stomach with the
pink strap of her nightgown meandering down her
shoulder. Her mouth is pressed open against the sheet;
her eyes are still closed. Her hair is matted against her
ear, half hidden by a pillow that has fallen partly over

her head. He watches his wife sleep, this woman he has lived with for fifteen years, watches her breathe, and as he does so, he feels again, as he has felt at odd moments over the past several weeks, the tremulous drag of guilt, a line snagged with seaweed. In a file cabinet in the room below the bedroom, there are in a manila folder six letters and a postcard that could not be easily explained, that are, in their seeming innocence, as treacherous as motel receipts. Yet he resists this drag of guilt, knows he cannot afford to let it take hold of him. Not today, not this morning.

He rolls over, squints at the clock. Nearly six forty-five. Christ, it has to have been the longest night of his life, and there are still five hours and fifteen minutes to go. He knows already that the morning is lost to him, held suspended in anticipation: Will she be there? Will she come at all? He has no reason to expect her. She has written that she wants it—the nebulous "it" they have created only with words—to stop, and he has ignored her. He's done worse than ignore her: He's sent her the goddamn tape!

He slips out from between the sheets, walks naked into the bathroom. The tile floor is ice against the soles of his feet, the air so frigid he begins almost immediately to shiver. He minds that he pays six hundred dollars a month for heat and can still see his breath in the morning. He turns on the shower, watches as clouds of steam boil over and around the plastic curtain. His face in the mirror disappears; the bathroom fills with mist. He steps into the shower, adjusts the water temperature so that it is just below scalding. He turns, bends his head, lets the water pummel the back of his neck.

It has not, he knows, been an innocent correspondence. In the beginning he tried to tell himself that it was harmless, simply intriguing, but he knew, even then, that from the very first sentence of the very first note, there was nothing innocent about it. If he wrote her, as he had, that he had the same feeling looking at her picture as he had when he first saw her in the courtyard of The Ridge thirty-one years ago, what did that imply? And although he has not permitted himself to think of Siân Richards sexually—he cannot, despite his childhood memories, despite the temptation, for to do so might allow the "it" to spiral out of control—he knows that however chaste his thinking is, it is not innocent. Not to have told his wife, to have shielded Siân's picture with his elbow, was to have given the "it" a life. He remembers sitting in the car at the beach that rainy Sunday afternoon, drafting and redrafting that first letter, trying to strike just the right chord, find the right tone—a tone somewhere between revelatory and careful—and how he waited for days after that, convinced that the letter had been lost in the mailroom of her publisher, that it had not been forwarded after all.

But then she had replied. He remembers still the delicate blue surprise of that letter, how his hand trembled as he withdrew the envelope with the unfamiliar hand from the postbox, how he sat outside in his car and opened it and read the letter, not once but many times, before he was calm enough to start the Cadillac and move away from the post office. Her handwriting was tiny, cramped, with the capitals strangely pointed, and he had to look at several words twice or three times before he could decipher them. But she had used the word "delighted," had remembered him as Cal. And at the end of the letter she had all but invited him to write to her again: If he knew what she looked like and what she did for a living, she said, oughtn't he then to tell her what he looked like and what he did for a living?

He got her letter on the twenty-fifth of September, had responded the next day. And then there was what seemed like an interminable wait for a subsequent letter. Each day he went to the post office, looked for the small, cramped penmanship. He thought of what he had written her, became convinced that something he said had put her off. Perhaps he'd been too forward, too bold. Too suggestive. Once, telling Harriet he had business in Boston, he got into the Cadillac and drove across Connecticut and New York and into Pennsylvania, to the town on the return address of Siân's envelope. He had no intention of making an unannounced visit; he simply wanted to see where she lived, as though from that he might derive more clues as to whom she had become. He knew, even as he was making the drive, that he was behaving like a teenager, not a grown man with a wife and three children, but he was unable convincingly to talk himself out of making the journey. (He thinks now, standing in the shower, perhaps that was the point of the trip after all: He was reliving something he hadn't been able to do as a teenager—the bike ride across three states.)

The trip through Connecticut and New York was exhilarating. He had Roy on the tape player and another tape he'd bought in September, in search of the song he remembered at the beach, a tape of golden oldies from what he had already come to think of as "their" era, and the day was fine. Crisp and golden, pure fall.

But he wasn't at all prepared for the sight of her town, stranded, it seemed from his vantage point as he followed the map across the border and over the mountain, amidst a vast black desert. He knew only from the poems that what he saw had to be the "black dirt" she wrote of; if it wasn't for the poetry, he'd have thought he'd spun off into the surreal, that the land west of the small mountain was sealed with tar, that he'd somehow stumbled upon a foreign landing strip. He descended the winding road cautiously and drove straight into the town, and as he did so he felt the exhilaration of the journey dissipating. The light over the black dirt was unearthly and pale, and even though the sun still shone, the houses looked washed out or smudged. He decided then that the effect was created by the blackness of the soil; the light was sucked up, he thought, swallowed by the dirt itself.

In the center of the small village was a dark Catholic church with a parking lot to one side and a cemetery in the back. Opposite the church was a row of storefronts—a video store, an uninviting bar with faded blue curtains covering the windows, a real estate agency, and a restaurant, The Onion Inn. He had a sandwich there, asked the waitress if she could direct him to the street he was looking for. He wondered, while he ate his sandwich at the bar of the inn, if he would know Siân Richards if she walked in now, if when their eyes met she would know him. He'd been replaying various scenarios for days, imagining their first encounter after thirty-one years. Sometimes he imagined kissing her before he even spoke to her. He examined every woman in the restaurant—those at the tables, those who entered while he sat there—but none of them remotely resembled Siân. He didn't know what he'd do if he did encounter her that afternoon. She'd have thought him deranged if she knew he'd driven more than four hours just to see the town in which she lived. And almost certainly that information would have frightened her off. Yet it was all he could do to refrain from asking the waitress if she was familiar with the name.

He followed the waitress's directions to the address he had asked about. The road wasn't hard to find; there were only three leading from the village—one to the north of the onion fields, one to the south, and one that seemed to bisect the dark desert like a canal. Hers was to the north, the farms arranged along it as along a shoreline. He drove by the house twice before he realized it was the address he wanted: The number was hidden from view behind a post on the front porch. It was a gray house with black shutters, a farmhouse with an ell. Out on the front lawn was an ancient elm, its leaves this time of year just beginning to catch fire. He saw, in the three or four times he passed the house after he realized which was hers, that there were white curtains at each of the windows, that the red barn in the back belonged to the farmhouse, and that there was a flower garden at the side. To the other side was a massive yellow tractor in the driveway. Each time he passed the house he slowed the car down and held his breath, wanting to see a woman and yet not wanting at all to see a woman, but there was no activity as he came and went—not a movement behind a window, not a child playing in the yard, not a man walking toward the barn. He'd wondered where she was, what precisely she was doing then.

Later, after he'd driven the other roads leading from the village and had seen all there was to see of the town—primarily other farmhouses, most of which had been painted in odd, pastel colors that seemed to obliterate whatever charm the buildings might intrinsically have had in some previous era—he crossed another small mountain in order to reach the university, and he had thought that the bleakness of the valley, however dispiriting (but was it bleakness, he wondered, or was it simply the fear of being swallowed up by the black dirt oneself?), was somehow encouraging: If he had discovered Siân Richards living in a pretty village, on a sunlit street, with a Volvo station wagon in the driveway and a ten-speed Motobecane on a front porch (or, worse, in an imposing fortress on Manhattan's East Side, with a doorman out front and a Porsche in a garage somewhere down below), might he not have felt more inhibited in his pursuit of their much-imagined reunion? And yet he had to concede as well that possibly Siân Richards was perfectly happy at her farm and in her marriage, that the despair suggested in her poetry—the suggestion of pinched lives—did not come from her own circumstances but was a metaphor for something larger, which he might better grasp if he knew more about poetry.

The university was a small one in population, though it did have a large agricultural school, and it was through fallow fields that Charles drove to reach the main campus. Classes were in session that day, and he wondered if Siân was there, teaching. He hadn't seen a car of any kind in the driveway of her house. He walked a series of footpaths under bare trees and between red-brick buildings until he had crisscrossed most of the central campus. Girls in thick sweaters and boys in neon parkas looked at him as they passed by. He studied each older woman he encountered—hopeful and panicky at once that he might stumble upon her. Occasionally his own years at Holy Cross came back to him. He was certain, when he left finally (too late to make it home in time for dinner, and he had to compose yet another lie in the car), that he had not come face-to-face with Siân Richards, though it was easier to imagine her there, on that campus, than it was to envision her in the gray house by the onion fields.

After that day, he developed a habit of going to the post office three, four times a day in search of a blue envelope in his box. For weeks, it seemed, there was nothing, and then finally she wrote him. Hers, he thought, was an odd correspondence, one that was, at its heart, not always easy to decipher. Sometimes she seemed encouraging; at other times, occasionally even in the same letter, she appeared to withdraw. It was a kind of feinting: a touch here, then a retreat. His own correspondence to her, he was certain, was not difficult to read. He was pushing her, he knew, even at the risk that she might close up altogether. He thought that he had taken a terrible leap by describing the "awful loneliness" of her poetry, but she hadn't seemed to mind that. And sometimes he thought he detected humor in her letters, as when she echoed his comment about her husband in her comment about his wife, or when she said thanks, but she wouldn't need a chaperone. (He imagined—hoped for?—a dry wit.) Yet she could unnerve him as well. She said that he would be disappointed when he met her. What did "disappointed" mean? he wondered for days.

And just at the point when he was poised to suggest the where and when of a meeting, she wrote that she was leaving for England. He was thrown into the unreasonable confusion of a teenage boy. It occurred to him when he got that letter that something was seriously wrong with him; it (again, the nebulous "it" they'd created—*he'd* created—only with words) was merely a fantasy, a figment of his imagination. How could he miss a woman he'd never even met? He'd met the child, the girl, but he couldn't say, in any lucid moment, that he knew the woman. And yet he remembers vividly the night he got her letter, how he walked outside into the backyard and looked up at the night sky with all its stars and imagined a jet taking her to England. And he wrote the next day that he missed her already. Surely that was madness.

But then there was the letter with the photograph, the one she found and sent to him before her plane was leaving. He'd been moved by the picture—it was one thing to remember himself as a child with her as a child; it was quite another actually to see the two of them together, with his arm around her, her eyes cast down, the two children clearly in the throes of some charged emotion—yet even more moved by the way in which she'd written about the photograph, by the very fact that she'd had to find the picture at all. Yes, it did mean that once they had been together, that she was, after all, just as he had imagined her. But didn't it also mean that she had needed to see some tangible proof as well?

From that he took encouragement and wrote her the longest letter, the one in which he told her he'd once fallen in love at first sight and that something similar may have happened when he saw her photograph three decades later; that he was looking for an "open connection"; that he wanted to hold her hand. And she wrote that she wanted him to stop. He had no choice then but to push blindly ahead, to ignore her request. He was, after all, a salesman. He had to be able to see her again.

Yet even so, he doesn't know if she will come today. It was risky to have arbitrarily set a day and time: What if she has a class? What if she's already arranged to be in the city with her publisher? He knows, however, that he has at least to try to meet her, to try to bring the "it" to fruition. He can no longer focus on his work; he hasn't been able to concentrate on his business for weeks now. He cannot somehow put aside the notion that meeting this woman is the single most important task he must accomplish, and he hopes (or is it that he fears?) that seeing her will somehow take the edge off—that Siân Richards in the flesh will dispel the fantasies he has created.

He emerges from the shower, and the tune and the words are still with him. He hums a bit, takes it to the end. The song is with him all the time now, sometimes as a repeated melody, sometimes as a code he cannot entirely crack. He knows he has sung it silently hundreds of times since September. After that afternoon at the beach, the afternoon when he first heard its echoes floating across thirty-one years, he sought it out, found it finally, as more phrases came back to him, on an old album in a secondhand-record store. The familiar rendition, he discovered, was by Dion & The Belmonts (he ought to have known that), but he is aware now that there have been many other versions, and he has unearthed some of them. The song is old, 1937, Rodgers and Hart. He remembers playing the 45 endlessly as a boy (that and its flip side, "That's My Desire") during the era he met Siân Richards—the song hit the charts in the summer of 1960, the summer they met at camp. He is puzzled now, however, by how the boy he was can have interpreted the lyrics, can have understood them at all, apart from the sense of pure longing. They seem almost to require the mystery of loss and rediscovery—states of being he can't possibly have been familiar with at fourteen.

Beyond his humming he can hear activity in the house. Harriet will be up now, will be negotiating the children through their breakfast. He wonders, not for the first time in the past several weeks, how his wife can have failed to notice his distraction. He hasn't slept or eaten well in days. He wipes the mirror of condensation, peers at his reflection. He looks like shit. His eyes are bloodshot from lack of sleep, the skin below them is wrinkled; he has bags under his eyes for the first time in his life. His hair is thinning, considerably more gray than brown now. He thinks of the tall boy with the crew cut in the photograph, the promise of that boy. Christ, couldn't this have happened to him when he was thirty-five, when he had all his hair and a flatter stomach? He looks more closely into the mirror, sees the beginning of a pimple under his cheekbone. That's all he needs. He shaves carefully, puts a Stridex tab on the incipient pimple. He brushes his teeth twice. He has planned to wear his gray suit, wonders now if that mightn't be too conservative. No, he'll stick with the gray suit, a white shirt, a dark tie. Keep it simple.

When he enters the kitchen, Harriet is at the counter, making school lunches; Hadley is thoughtfully working her way through an English muffin. She has a textbook open beside her. She is the only one of the three children who resembles him—wide brown eyes, prominent ears, straight teeth, slightly off center, light brown hair as his once was. He feels the guilt again, the seaweed. He pours himself a cup of coffee, sits across from Hadley. He asks her what she's reading; she looks up at him and answers, Geography, a test. Like him, Hadley has always been an early riser and even as a small child dressed herself and was down for breakfast before any of the others. He thinks of her, too, as the most responsible of the three, though that might simply be her age. He cannot say, however, that he loves her more than he loves the other two; he has never been able to compartmentalize his love like that, to feel more for one than for the others. His love for them is of a piece, and that is how he thinks of it—a vast, diffuse, protective warmth that surrounds and envelops all of them.

Harriet asks him from the counter what his day will be like, a question she asks him nearly every morning so as to determine better the shape of her own day, and he tells her, as he has rehearsed, that he will be away in Boston, two clients and a late lunch, and as he does so it seems to him that his voice thins out, that the sentences sound not only rehearsed but also blatantly untruthful. He watches for a sign that she has perceived the falsehood—a shift of her head, a tensing of her shoulders—but instead she deftly slices three sandwiches, packs them into plastic bags. He is aware of the heat in his face, and when he turns to Hadley he sees that she is staring at him. He smiles at her, takes a sip of coffee.

"I'm off, then," he says. "Just get some papers."

He pushes his chair into the table, bends over and kisses his daughter. Harriet does not turn around.

Some years ago he gave up the custom of kissing his wife when he left the house. He cannot now remember what year it was, though he remembers well the morning he decided to forgo the ritual. He had passed through the kitchen and was standing at the door when he realized he could not possibly walk the seven or eight steps to his wife at the sink, could not experience again the reflexive and pursed pecking at the mouth, their bodies not touching, as if they were birds, or distant, strained siblings. And oddly, though he watched for some sign of unease on her part and was prepared to resume the custom if she pressed him, she seemed not to mind the lapse at all, nor even to notice that they no longer touched outside of the bedroom. He sometimes wonders guiltily what messages they are giving their children by never being demonstrative, but it seems to him a small, forgivable parental transgression that he lacks the will to do much about now.

He leaves the kitchen and walks into the office, the old front room, a room now swimming in papers, unopened boxes, and electronic equipment, a room too small to absorb the contents of the building he once called his office and has now irretrievably lost. He puts a sheaf of random papers into a briefcase, tucks his briefcase under his arm, walks again through the kitchen. He takes his topcoat from a clothes tree in the corner and watches as Harriet turns, gives a small wave with her hand. Have a good day, she says, and smiles, and he says back to her, You too. He does not look again at his daughter.

Outside, the day is gray and raw, not unusual for the

first week of December, but disappointing to Charles, who has wanted sunshine, some bright omen. He has planned his route—west on 95, north on 7—and it should take him just under three hours. He'll be there before ten, but that's all right. He needs to see the place, walk around, gather his wits before she comes.

He puts a tape, *the* tape, into the tape deck. He's made a duplicate of the one he sent Siân. He has in his office dozens of rejects—tapes on which the sequence wasn't perfect, on which there were gaps that weren't acceptable, on which he'd put songs he decided wouldn't do after all. At first he was tickled by the project, then he became obsessed. He sequestered himself each evening in his study with his turntable and his tape player, listening to albums and 45s he'd found in old record stores, sifting through his own albums. He spent hours with his Sony in quiet bars, hunting down old tunes on jukeboxes. Astonishingly Harriet did not ask him once what he was doing in his study in the evenings (what can she possibly have thought of the music emanating from the room night after night?), though she has mentioned once or twice that she is concerned about his "stress level."

Then he actually sent the tape, the small player, and the headphones. It was the most reckless gesture of all, one he regretted the minute he watched Harry Noonan behind the counter at the post office toss it into the Priority Mail bucket. He expected the box back unopened almost immediately, dreaded going to the post office each day and finding the little pink slip announcing that there was a package waiting for him. He was positive, too, that the picture he sent along with the package, the picture of him holding the fish, was going to backfire. It was a terrible picture, but it was the only one he could find that showed him alone—without one of his children or Harriet.

He listens to the first song on the tape, Dion's "A Teenager in Love." He has tried, in the correspondence, for a tone of lightheartedness, and he sent the tape in the same vein, though he is certain—and he suspects this has been all too obvious to her as well—that his entire life hangs in the balance of her response. He *has* felt like a schoolboy, a teenager, with a teenager's innocence and longing.

He is confident, too, though he understands this less well, that she has been there all along, all through the years, a kind of subterranean rhythm or current. He knows this because he has always favored women who looked like Siân—tall, small-breasted, blondish (and it has often puzzled him that he married a woman so unlike this image)—and he knows Siân was the first, the antecedent. And her name, her strange Welsh name, has bubbled up into his consciousness over the years, often when he has least expected it. In college, he roomed for a year with a boy named Shane, and he frequently slipped and called him Sean, the spelling different but the pronunciation the same as hers. He remembers, also, a client he had seven or eight years ago, a Susan Wain, and how he twice addressed correspondence to her, Dear Sian, without the accent, somehow transposing letters subconsciously from the last name to the first, but again echoing the antecedent. He hadn't realized his mistake until the client pointed it out to him.

He knows as well that through the years he has been drawn to things Welsh, a subconscious draw, as if one were trying to find something lost in childhood—a piece of music, the shape of a room, the way the light once filtered through a certain window. He remembers reading Dylan Thomas and Chatwin's *On the Black Hill* not too long ago, and another book, Jan Morris's *The Matter of Wales*, and deciding that if he ever got to Europe he might begin with Wales and then make his way south to Portugal. (Though when he drives to the beach and looks out, he never imagines looking at Wales—it's too far *north*, he thinks.) He will have to ask her, but he thinks he has remembered this correctly, that she has a Welsh father and had an Irish mother, both first-generation immigrants after World War II, and though there was no lilt in her own voice, as there was in her father's (he remembers the father's accent vividly from that phone call he made when he had returned home from college: the strange vowels, the crescendo and sudden swift fall in the rhythm of the sentences), it was evident, looking at her (particularly on that first day at camp and, more recently, even in the photograph in the newspaper), that she had Celtic origins. It is in the shape of the mouth possibly, or in the high forehead, or perhaps it is the eyes with their pale eyebrows.

The second song is on now: "Angel Baby," Rosie & The Originals. He loves Rosie's nasal twang, is not sure they ever had another hit. Great slow beat on this one, though. For months after they left each other at camp, he and Siân corresponded. He wonders if she might still have those old letters—hers to him, he knows, were lost when his parents' basement was flooded and everything that had been stored there for him was destroyed. He doesn't now know why the correspondence ended; he suspects it began to seem more and more hopeless as the months wore on. He had thought and planned endlessly, he remembers, to find a way to see her again, and these adolescent schemes now seem comical and sad to him. How ever was a fourteen-year-old boy to make his way across three states to see his girlfriend? At that age, one was prisoner of one's parents. He certainly had no car, did not even know anyone with a car except for people his parents' age, none of whom was likely to drive him to Springfield, Massachusetts, from Bristol, Rhode Island. If only he and Siân had met at sixteen, when seeing her again, seeing her continuously over the years, might have been possible.

He turns up the volume. He loves this one: "That's My Desire." He waits each time for the falsetto at the end, sometimes tries to imitate it himself. He remembers as vividly as if it were yesterday the agony of that final and irrevocable separation, the anticipation of that separation all that last morning of camp and, indeed, even the entire day before. If one week at camp were the experiential equivalent of a lifetime together, then the last day and a half has to have taken on, in the savoring of each minute, the totality of years.

He woke that last morning with a strange feeling in

his stomach, a mixture of dread and guilt and deep sexual excitement. (Odd how clearly he can remember this—more clearly, it seems to him, than more recent events, from college or from seminary, or even from the early years of his marriage.) He'd had a counselor (what was his name?) who played 45s on a turntable in the boys' dorm. Johnny Mathis at night to soothe the overheated psyches of adolescent boys; The Silhouettes and The Shirelles in the morning to wake them up. "Get a Job" was on that morning. He'd woken after a restless night, a night full of wild dreams and schemes, as if he were a prisoner of war planning their escape—his and Siân's. He imagined hiding in the woods until all the parents had left, and then he and Siân would get on a bus. He had no idea where the bus might take them—he hadn't been able quite to make that work, and that was the point at which he'd begun to panic: Where could they go? What would they do for money? How long could they hide out from their parents or from the police? He smiles now to think of that boy, of his frantic and desperate imaginings.

He met her that morning in the dining hall. They'd sat at the same table all week. She was next to him, the bracelet on her wrist. She didn't speak. He remembers that she was wearing Bermuda shorts and a white blouse, a sleeveless blouse. Neither of them could eat. She'd pushed her eggs around; he hadn't even been able to do that. He'd sat with his fork in his hand, unable to speak to her in front of the others, unable to move. He wanted to touch the bracelet on her wrist, touch the hairs on her arm. To his right, on the other side of him, was his counselor (what *was* his name?), a big guy with a crew cut and a short-sleeved dress shirt that showed his muscles. They'd had to wear white shirts, he remembers that. He also remembers that his counselor had seemed unreasonably happy that morning, and Charles (Cal then) had formed an instant and lasting hatred for the man.

(It strikes him suddenly, as he engages the cruise control in his car, that the counselor was probably only a kid, a college kid then, someone he'd now think of as a child, and that at this point in time the man has to be in his early fifties at least.)

There was a blue plaid tablecloth on the table, heavy white crockery at each place. Prayers were said before the meal, and then again at the end. Siân had pushed her chair back; Charles was paralyzed with confusion. All he could think was that he and she would never share a meal together again. Very shortly they would never do anything together again at all. He had to be with her, had to be alone with her again, before they said goodbye.

He stood and asked her if she had packed. She said yes, looked down at her feet. She was wearing sneakers, he remembers, and no socks. Though she was tall, she had small feet. White sneakers. White Keds.

All week he had been with this girl as he had never been with anyone before—not his mother, not his father, not his best friend, Billy Cowan. How could he allow this person to be taken away from him? And why could he find no words at that moment to tell her what he felt, what he wanted?

And then she'd spoken, a miracle, a deft slip through the knot of his inexperience: Would he like to play badminton? she had asked. They could skip chapel just the once on this last day and play badminton before the parents came, before they had to leave. Just the two of them . . .

There it is now. "Where or When." *The* song. (Their song?) He'd planned it fourth, like a clean-up batter. The song is sung almost entirely a cappella. He listens to the whole of it, rewinds the tape, plays it again, as he almost always does. He plays the entire tape (fifteen songs) twice through, then turns the tape deck off. He chooses silence over the radio. He cannot focus on the news and doesn't want to hear any other music just now. He hasn't been able to read a newspaper in days, hasn't watched a television program with any kind of concentration since he saw her picture. He has to get this meeting over with, he knows, if only to return to some kind of normalcy.

He follows the map, the directions that were sent to him from The Ridge. The town in which the inn is located is in northwestern Connecticut, close to the new York border. He finds the town, drives with the directions between his thumb and the steering wheel. The town itself is a New England classic, recently refurbished, he suspects, during the boom of the eighties, the broad High Street lined with eighteenth-century three-story houses, all white, all with black shutters, all set back from the street, with well-manicured lawns leading to the front porches. (From force of habit, he counts the number of For Sale signs—seven in five blocks.) The inn, however, is at the outskirts of town, on the edge of a private lake. He discovers the road just south of the town park. A discreet sign indicating The Ridge with an arrow—carved gold letters on dark green—tells him that he's made the correct turn. He hopes that Siân, too, will see the small sign.

The houses dwindle in number as he drives; the inn appears to be at least five miles from the village center. The day is still damp and overcast, though not as chilly as it was earlier in the morning. Driving through town, he noticed a liquor store and a deli. After he locates The Ridge, he wants to pick up a bottle of champagne, a six-pack, and some ice. He has the cooler in the trunk, put it there last night after Harriet went to bed. He is not quite sure exactly how this will work, but he somehow envisions himself and Siân sharing a glass of champagne together on the grounds of The Ridge, or possibly in his car, before they go in to lunch. He would rather meet her that way, would rather have a drink alone with her, than greet her for the first time in a formal dining room, with waiters hovering.

He reaches the end of the road, comes to a stone wall with an open wrought-iron gate. Another sign in green and gold announces that he has arrived. He turns into a twisting drive of brick herringbone. Bare plane trees line the drive at precisely spaced intervals.

He has always known that the mansion and the grounds, before they were an inn or a camp, were privately held. He remembers now that the money came from shoes in the 1920s and that the last owner, sometime in the early 1950s, died and willed it to the Catholic Church. He wonders if the church owns the inn.

The long drive takes him through a thicket of birches, then opens to a panorama of the main house itself, behind a maze of formal gardens. He slows the car to a stop.

It's exactly the same. Nothing ever stays the same, he is thinking, but somehow this has done so. Amazingly, astonishingly, the estate is as he has remembered it.

He puts the car in gear, slips it into a parking space at the side of the inn. With some difficulty, as if he had suddenly aged, he steps from the car.

The house is a well-proportioned three-story building in gray stone, with wings to either side. The roof is slate, a greenish-gray, and the shutters at the windows are a faded pale blue, so faded and so pale they seem almost colorless, and he remembers with a clarity that startles him that they were nearly colorless even then, when the estate was a camp. They remind him now, as they cannot have reminded him then, of the shutters on French country houses in paintings and in photographs. The wings of the house are set at an angle so that they embrace a center courtyard of square, hand-cut stones. Frost and time have heaved some of the stones, and wisely no one has tampered with the uneven surface. In the center of the courtyard is the fountain—a patinaed bronze well with a graceful arc of water into which he tossed pennies and wishes as a child.

There are no signs in the courtyard or at the front

door, nothing to indicate that the camp of his memories has been transformed into an inn.

He looks out to the west wing, where the boys slept. He can see his room, the fourth window to the left on the top floor. He shared it with three other boys. A waiter in a black tuxedo emerges from the front door, nods at Charles, and makes his way across the court-yard to a door at the end of the east wing. A gust of wind comes from behind Charles, makes a swirl of dry leaves eddy in a corner. At a window on the second floor of the east wing, a curtain is drawn.

Charles hikes the collar of his navy wool coat, puts his hands into his pockets. A wash of light, the sun through a break in the clouds, moves swiftly across the facade of the house, then disappears.

$\mathcal{T}$he girl arrived first. She had her parents with her and one hard blue suitcase. She held the suitcase in front of her with two hands and walked from the car to the courtyard, where she had been told to go. She put the suitcase down beside her and stood near the front door, on the uneven stones. Her parents, curious, wanted to explore and left her alone. She herself was not anxious to explore; she knew that by evening the place would be known to her. She held her hands loosely clasped and stood quietly, watching the others arrive with their parents. She was wearing a blue dress, a thin cotton dress that fell just below her knees. She had worn the dress because her mother had insisted, but as she watched the others enter the courtyard, she saw that the girls were dressed in shorts and sleeveless blouses. Her hair, which was long that summer, was pulled back into a ponytail, yet even so, she was uncomfortably warm. It was the beginning of summer, midday, and the sun beat down upon the courtyard. Overhead, the sky was a deep blue and cloudless. She was wishing that all the parents would leave so that she could change her clothes. She was thinking about a swim. There was a lake, she had been told, and a pool, and even if the lake was not for swimming, she knew it would be cooler down by the water's edge.

When the boy arrived, he, too, was carrying his own suitcase, though he was tall enough and strong enough to hold it in one hand. He walked to the center of the courtyard, his parents behind him. His mother wore red lipstick and sunglasses with white frames. Her dress had a wide white collar, and she was having trouble on the stones with her high heels. His father was a tall man, with broad shoulders beneath his suit coat and a summer tan on his face and neck and wrists. His mother lit a cigarette, and even from across the courtyard, she could see the red lipstick mark on the mother's cigarette. The mother examined the families in the courtyard and turned to her husband with commentary behind her white-gloved hand. The boy stood still, in the center of the courtyard. He had on a white shirt, the sleeves rolled to the elbows, and a pair of black chinos. He wore black shoes, dress shoes, the sort a boy then would wear to mass. He had his hands in the pockets of his pants, and on his wrist she saw the silver glint of a watchband. There were perhaps twenty or thirty other people in the courtyard.

When he turned his head in her direction and looked at her for the first time, she did not glance away. He had soft brown eyes and a crew cut, and like his father, he had a summer tan. Her own face, she knew was white; her skin would not brown no matter how much oil she used. The boy looked at the girl for a long time, and she thought that possibly he smiled—a shy, nervous, unpracticed smile. He looked at the girl for so long that his mother noticed and turned to see who or what had caught her son's attention. And when the mother examined the girl—a frank stare of examination—the girl blushed finally and turned her head away.

Years later, I looked in the mirror and I thought: I cannot let him see this aging body.

In Africa, the sun had scalded my skin and left a residue of spots and wrinkles. I had a belly with a scar from a cesarean. My breasts were small, they had always been small, but there was no girl left; I had nursed two babies. My hair was graying at the sides.

Sometimes, when I was with you, I felt betrayed by my body.

When I drove to The Ridge, I played the tape loudly to drown out my imaginings. When I came into the parking lot, "Crying" was on, announcing me.

I saw the building with the blue shutters, and I thought: We were only children.

I emerged from my car, and I noticed, across the parking lot, a large American car, the sort of car I would not know, might not ever look at. The door opened, and a man got out. He had on a navy coat, a dark suit. His hair was graying, thinning at the top. His face had an elegant line. His body seemed elongated, and his gestures, as he shut the door, were poised. I was thinking of photographs of T. S. Eliot and of Scott Fitzgerald. I was thinking: Someone from another era, another decade.

The man looked at me, and I turned away.

Down at the lake, the wind rippled the water so that it appeared to be moving, one large body of water, like a river, moving. The lake was gray, and the sky; the trees had lost their leaves.

We sat on the wooden bench in our coats, side by side, and watched the water moving. And it seemed to us that what we saw that day was time.

❧ ❧ ❧ ❧ ❧ ❧

IT IS ONE MINUTE PAST NOON WHEN THE SMALL BLACK car—a Volkswagen Rabbit?—makes its way along the drive. The car executes what seems to be a practiced turn into the parking lot, comes to an abrupt stop. It *is* a VW, perhaps five years old. A woman is behind the wheel—a woman his age, and he has just the briefest sense of prettiness, in her profile, in her chin—and his heart leaps. But from her short, quick gestures as she emerges from the car, snaps the door to, and locks it, he thinks: Someone who works here, the hostess perhaps. He opens his own door, turns toward the VW, and stands, but the woman's face and body are a blur as she spins away from him. She wears a long black coat over what appears to be a suit, and she has on dark glasses despite the overcast day. He can see black high heels, a pocketbook slung over her shoulder. The hair may be the right color, though—a kind of dark blond with just a hint of red—and the woman wears it up, pinned back at the nape of her neck. It could conceivably be she, he thinks. He watches as she walks without much hesitation to the entrance of the inn. She disappears inside the building.

The heavy door opens to a long foyer tiled in black and white squares, in the center of which is a highly polished wooden staircase. He remembers the staircase now; it was on its wide steps each night that the entire camp, the children and the counselors, assembled for an event called "Stairway Sing" just before bedtime.

He opens large glass French doors to the left and to the right of the foyer and finds unoccupied sitting rooms. He then remembers that the dining room is at the top of the stairs; his memory is jogged when he hears sounds tinkling down the stairway. He climbs the stairs, his hand on the banister, a serious knot beginning in his stomach.

On the landing, he is aware of an abundance of brass and wood, thick white paint, massive bouquets of freesias and lilies, a rose Oriental at his feet. A small, thin man in a tuxedo offers to take his coat. As Charles turns obligingly, pulling his arm from the sleeve, he sees her standing by the maître d's desk. She is watching him speculatively, making no sign or gesture to commit herself. She has on a black suit with a white blouse, a silk blouse with soft folds along its deep neckline. He can see the bones of her clavicle, and a thin gold chain around her neck. She has on her sunglasses still, but he recognizes the gold earrings, simple circles, heavy gold circles at her earlobes.

"Siân?"

His voice cracks slightly on the name, as if he has not spoken in some time. He clears his throat.

She tilts her head.

"Charles?"

She takes the dark glasses off, allowing his scrutiny. Her eyes are nearly navy, with flecks of gold, and he remembers that now, the contrast, almost startling, of the dark eyes with the pale skin. There are wrinkles at the corners of her eyes and below them, but her forehead is unlined—high and white and unlined. He pauses at her mouth.

"I'd have worn the bracelet," she says, "as a sign. But I ran out of time and couldn't find it."

She smiles, her lips together, and tilts her head again, as if questioning him, or waiting. She is tall in heels, nearly as tall as he is. He supposes she is five nine, five ten in stocking feet, the length of her, he can see at once, in her legs. The skirt she is wearing is simple and straight, falling slightly above the knee.

But her voice is new to him. As he knows his must be to her. In their voices they must be strangers. He wonders if his voice had already changed when he met her, or was changing that summer. Her voice is deeper than he expected. She speaks slowly.

"I didn't need the bracelet," he says.

It seems she smiles again, glances in the direction of the maître d', who has been waiting behind Charles. Charles, feeling that he must gather himself together and take charge somehow, gives the man his name, says nonsmoking when he is asked, then wonders. He turns to her, but she shakes her head. He thinks of his mother, smoking in automobiles with the windows shut tight. He waits while she puts the dark glasses into her pocketbook, takes out another pair of glasses, clear glasses with thin wire frames. She removes them from their case and puts them on. He did not know she wore glasses, and he tries to remember if she had them when they were children. Thinks now that she may have, though she almost never wore them.

He follows her through the dining room, his breathing tight, his heart missing beats. Other diners look up at her when she passes, in the way that people notice a tall woman walking through a room. The maître d' leads them to a banquette against one wall. He pulls the table out, gestures for her to sit. Charles sits beside her, turning his body slightly in her direction. He lays his arm along the back cushion of the banquette. She seems uneasy with the side-by-side arrangement, crosses her legs. Her skirt rides up slightly on her thigh. He allows his eyes momentarily to fall on the span between her knees and the hemline of her skirt. Her stockings are sheer, with a dark tint. He orders a Stoli martini, bone dry, with a twist, and wishes he could inject it. She orders a glass of wine.

"The tape," she says. "At first I didn't want it. I didn't want you to be sending me things. But last night I listened to it finally. It was . . ."

She stops, unable to find the word.

He waits, and when she doesn't finish the sentence, he says, "It was meant to be lighthearted. A joke. Kind of."

He thinks it may have been partially intended as

lighthearted, but he knows and he knows she knows, its true intent was something larger and deeper.

"I hadn't heard any of those songs in years," she says. "They . . ." She puts her fingers to the gold chain at her neck. "It was a kind of excavation. I felt it as that." She looks down, as if she may already have said too much.

"This is very strange," she says.

"It certainly is."

"Can you remember it? What do you remember?"

"I remember some things," he says. "Some things very vividly. Other parts are a blur now."

A waiter arrives with the drinks. Charles picks up his glass, swirls the ice, takes a swallow. He watches as she brings her glass to her lips, pauses, then looks at him. She moves her glass in his direction.

"To . . .?"

He does not hesitate. "Reunions," he says.

"And time passing," she adds, nearly as quickly.

He nods. He catches her eyes as they both simultaneously take sips of their drinks. When they are finished, he says, recklessly: "To the next thirty-one years."

She seems startled. As if there were no reply to this. She surveys the room. "I was surprised," she says, "that the place is so unchanged. I thought somehow it would be different."

He studies her profile, the same profile he saw briefly in the car. It has always intrigued him how much one can tell about a person with one quick glance at a profile—age mostly, also weight, sometimes ethnic background. Her profile is classic, but she is not a classic beauty, he thinks, and he suspects she probably never was, the forehead too high, the eyebrows too pale. Yet he is certain he has never seen a more arresting mouth. And he doesn't know if this is because it is a feature he has remembered all these years, the prototype by which he subconsciously judged others; would he find it so if he met her today for the first time? Her neck is long and white. Closer to her now, he can see that there are small discolorations, like freckles but not, on the backs of her hands and inside the neckline of her blouse. Her nails are short, unpainted. Like him, she wears a wedding ring.

He examines the dining room with her. To one side are floor-to-ceiling windows that, he knows from memory, give onto a sloping lawn leading down to the lake. The windows are arched at the top and let in a diffuse light that spreads across the room. The ceiling is high, vaulted, with fading cherubs depicted in blue-and-peach mosaics. He remembers now that there were jokes at dinner about the naked cherubs. When they were children, they ate at refectory tables—eight, ten, twelve to a table. The chairs scraped the floor. Now there are banquettes against the south wall, small dining tables covered with heavy damask linen, upholstered chairs in red-and-white-striped silk. There are white flowers in delicate vases on each of the tables.

"Do you suppose the food is any good?" she asks.

"It can't help but be an improvement over what we ate when we were here last."

She smiles.

"It was actually kind of a classy camp, I think now," he says. "As camps go."

"Yes, it was," she answers. "Though I don't suppose we knew enough then to appreciate the fact."

"I don't think I noticed much of anything then," he says, "apart from you."

He lets his hand slip off the banquette cushion and rest on her shoulder, the shoulder closest to him, and as he does so he can feel her stiffen. The touch to him is momentous, charged, the first touch since he last saw her. Of course, she is a stranger to him, a woman he has known only minutes; and yet he is certain he has known the girl forever.

He removes his hand.

He wonders, briefly, if she might be reticent about physical love, and then he has, almost simultaneously, another thought, an unwelcome one, a way to measure out the time lost, the thirty-one years, the measurement being the sum total of all the sexual experiences she has had, all the boyfriends, all the nights with her husband. The realization buffets him, makes him slightly ill, so that when she speaks, he has to ask her to repeat the sentence.

"Tell me about your wife," she says again. She reaches forward to the table, picks up her glass as if to take a sip.

He stalls, still awash in the confusion of his previous thought. He thinks about her question and then understands that it is for the hand on her shoulder. He drains the vodka, bites into the lemon peel. "She has short, dark hair," he says. He hesitates; he feels lost. "She's a good person," he says lamely.

"Do you love her?"

He pauses. He must get this right. He must not lie. He senses she will know a lie. He swirls the ice cubes and the lemon peel in his glass. "I love her more than I used to," he says slowly and deliberately.

She brings the glass to her lips, as if pondering his reply. As he looks at her, the space between them becomes flooded with images: the two of them as children; the picture she sent him; the girl she might have been at seventeen; the woman she might have been at twenty-eight or thirty-five; herself in the embrace of another man—her husband? Her husband, about whom he knows almost nothing but who almost certainly has more hair than Charles does and probably (Charles winces inwardly) a flatter stomach. He imagines her lying on a bed with her hair undone. He sees her nursing an infant. The images elide and collide. He feels light-headed, signals the waiter for another vodka.

"Do you want another glass of wine?" he asks her, and she surprises him by finishing her drink and nodding.

"It's hard to take it all in, isn't it?" she says. She shakes her head slightly, as if she truly cannot digest the fact, as if, like him, she can barely believe she's been alive thirty-one years, let alone known someone that long. Though of course they haven't known each other, he thinks.

He looks out at the other diners in the restaurant: a table of businessmen, several tables of couples, mostly older couples. The waiter brings them menus, recites the specials of the day. Charles dutifully listens to the man, as does she, but for his part he cannot absorb a word. He won't be able to read the menu either—he's left his reading glasses in the car.

"Are you hungry?" he asks her when the waiter has left.

She shakes her head.

"You're right," he says. "You don't look like your picture."

She seems embarrassed. "I think they were trying to make me out to be more interesting and glamorous than I really am," she says with a wave of her hand.

"That's not what I meant," he says. "I meant you look more familiar to me now than you did in the picture. You look very familiar to me."

She turns away from him toward the waiter across the room. "Oh, I almost forgot," she says. "I've brought something. I found it in the trunk with the pictures."

She bends down to retrieve her purse, a black leather pocketbook with a long strap, opens it, and removes a mimeographed newsletter, several pages stapled at one corner. She hands it to Charles.

"It was a kind of newspaper they gave us on the day we left. It has a brief history of what happened that week, and at the end there are all the addresses of the campers and the counselors."

Charles riffles through the newsletter, looks again at its cover, at the hand-drawn cross with the words "The Ridge" above it, and the dates of their attendance below. He puts the newsletter on the banquette between them.

"I've left my reading glasses in the car," he says.

"It's odd," she says, "but I don't recognize a single name there, except yours."

Her eyelids are slightly hooded; a soft tint in her glasses takes the edge off the navy of her eyes, makes them appear almost charcoal. She wears little makeup, at least as far as he can tell, and there is just the faintest suggestion of a dark rose color on her lips. He knows he should ask about her husband, as she has asked about his wife. And there are facts he would like to know about her marriage, though not necessarily from her. He does not want to hear her speak of her husband—not today, not right now.

"You certainly don't look like the wife of a farmer," he says lightly.

She laughs for the first time. "Well, you don't look like a salesman," she says.

"What's a salesman look like?" he asks. He would like to ask her what she thinks of him—has he aged hopelessly? is she disappointed?—but, of course, he cannot.

She glances again at the newsletter with the cross. "I don't remember much religion from that week," she says. "It's strange when you think about it. Except for the epiphany I wrote you about, and the services down by the water. Though they seem, at least in my memory, not very Catholic. Not very ornate. Having more to do with nature than with God."

He thinks this is true. There was a priest, he recalls, a tall, athletic fellow with thick black hair—Father Something: Father What?—who doubled as a swimming teacher. A number of lay counselors. Not a single nun.

"What was the priest's name?" he asks.

She thinks a minute. "Father Dunn?" she asks tentatively.

He smiles. "Thank you. You're right. They soft-pedaled the religion. Mercifully. And wisely too."

"I remember the pool, but I didn't see it on my way in."

"We can take a walk," he says.

She shifts lightly, moving her shoulder away. As if she might not acquiesce to a walk.

"You don't look like a poet either," he says. "Though I don't really know what a poet is supposed to look like."

Her hand is on the banquette, resting there between them. He covers her hand with his own.

The room spins for a second, as if he were already drunk.

"Does this upset you?" he asks her quietly. She shakes her head but doesn't look at him.

They sit there for minutes. She seems unwilling to withdraw her hand; he is unable to remove his. He feels the warmth of her hand beneath his, though he is barely touching her. He sees the waiter across the room. He will kill the man if he comes to their table now.

When she speaks, her voice is so low he is not sure he has heard her correctly.

"When you wrote about holding my hand . . ."

He waits, poised for the conclusion of the sentence. He rubs the top of her hand lightly.

She leans slightly toward him, an infinitesimal, yet highly significant, millimeter closer. She looks down at his hand over hers. She slips her hand from his, but gives her face to him. Her eyes are clear, unclouded.

"I had a son," she says quickly. "He was killed in a car accident when he was nine."

"I'm sorry," Charles says.

"His name was Brian. It was six years ago."

She tells him these facts in a steady voice, as if she had planned to tell him, as if she could not proceed without his knowing. He feels then the full weight of all that each of them has lived through, all of the separate minutes she has had to experience, to endure. The time they have been away from each other has been a lifetime—a lifetime of other people, other loves, sexual love, children, work. She has had to bury a child. He can barely imagine that pain. They once knew each other for one week; they have not seen each other in three decades. The imbalance staggers him.

"I'm not hungry either," he says quietly. "Why don't we get our coats and walk down to the lake. We can always eat later if we want to."

She opens her mouth as if to speak, closes it. She seems to be trying to tell him something, but cannot. She touches the back of his hand on the banquette lightly, briefly, with her fingertips.

He places the coat over her shoulders. She wraps herself in it as if it were a cape. In the foyer, he finds the door to the back, the one leading down to the lake. When she steps outside, she pulls the coat around her more tightly. The breeze is stiffer here, the day still overcast and cold. They hear a windowpane rattling. The wind loosens her hair a bit, makes stray wisps at the sides.

He has his arm at her back, guiding her across a wide stone porch.

"Wait here a minute," he says. "You'd probably rather have a thermos of hot coffee right now, but I brought something to celebrate our reunion."

When he walks to the car, his legs feel loose, boneless. He's aware he's moving too quickly, but he does not want to leave her alone, even for a minute, as if, after so brief a reunion, she might disappear again. He has few conscious thoughts, no plans. In his ears there is a pounding, a kind of desperate beat. His fingers tremble as he unlocks the trunk. The glasses are plastic, bought in the deli. He minds now that he didn't think to bring champagne glasses.

When he returns, she is standing at the edge of the porch, leaning against a stone railing, looking down toward the lake. She has the collar of her coat up, her arms wrapped around her. Before her, there is a sloping lawn, then a thicket of trees. Beyond the trees, they can see the far edge of the lake, a thin silver oval.

"The path is here somewhere," he says.

"Yes, I remember it."

"Can you manage in those shoes?"

"I think so. I can give it a try anyway."

She puts her hand on the railing, balances herself as

she descends the stairs. She has a slight limp, and she explains: "My knee. From a skiing accident."

(He adds then another image to his mental collage— she's in a ski outfit, her poles dug into the snow. But whom is she with? Her husband? A friend?)

He walks slightly behind her and to her right, the bottle in one hand, the glasses in the other.

"Do you think they mind us drinking our own champagne," she asks over her shoulder, "walking all over their property?"

"This is America. We can do anything we want."

She looks at him and smiles. They are on the lawn, and he is at her side. She seems brighter now, more relaxed, the sadness in the restaurant momentarily dissipated.

"Well, we know that's not true," she says quickly. "I hope you're not going to tell me you're a Republican."

"I knew you were going to ask me that. Is it important?"

"Yes, of course it's important."

"Well, I've never voted, so I guess that lets me off the hook."

"You've never voted?"

"And another thing you're going to hate."

"What's that?"

"I drive a Cadillac."

The backs of her heels are sinking into the lawn. When they reach the lake he will offer to clean them for her.

"So it was you in the parking lot," she says.

He laughs. "You looked right at me. I couldn't believe

you looked at me and walked so quickly away. I thought I'd scared you off."

"Well, I didn't really look at you, and even if I'd known it was you, I can promise you there wasn't a chance on God's earth I was going to walk across that parking lot and introduce myself."

"I thought you were the hostess."

She seems taken aback. "The hostess?"

"You drove in so quickly, as if you were late for work. As if you knew the place."

"I was just nervous."

"Why?"

They reach the pathway in the woods, the one that will lead them down to what was the outdoor chapel by the lake.

"I was just about to call you *Cal*," she says. "It's hard to think of you as Charles now. I had the tape on. Roy Orbison. 'Crying.' A wonderful song."

"He not only sang all those songs, but he also wrote most of them."

"I don't know much about that music. But I do remember it."

"I went to a concert of his once. In Providence. An incredible concert. Now, there was a man with a lot of pain in his life. He was riding motorcycles with his wife, and his wife was hit and killed instantly. And I think he lost at least one and possibly two sons in a fire."

As soon as he has spoken, he realizes what he has said. She is in front of him, walking single file along the path, watching her feet so that she will not stumble.

"Jesus Christ," he says. "I'm sorry."

She shrugs slightly as if to say it doesn't matter. They walk along the path in silence for perhaps a hundred yards. Overhead are tall pines, their tops swaying in the wind. Down below, on the path, it is quiet, with few sounds—the rustle of an animal in the bushes, a flock of geese he can hear flying and calling somewhere out of sight.

They emerge to a clearing of simple rough-hewn wooden benches on a carpet of pine needles. The clearing opens to the lake, an expansive view across gray rippling water. In the center of the clearing, at the edge of the lake, is the place where the cross—a wooden cross vaguely a man's height—used to be.

"I remember this," she says beside him.

He steps ahead of her and walks to the bench closest to the lake. He sits down and looks out. He puts the two plastic glasses on the bench, works the top of the champagne bottle. She sits, her hands in the pockets of her coat, on the other side of the glasses. The cork pops, flies toward the lake. He catches the spill of champagne in a glass, hands it to her. He fills the other glass, takes a sip. He wants to make another toast, looks out at the water instead. The water seems to be moving, an optical illusion. He wants to say the word "destiny" but does not. He remembers their sitting there as children, can remember holding her hand as if it were yesterday—the deep, sexual thrill of that gesture.

"What I tried to tell you in the restaurant and couldn't," she says, breaking the silence, "is that somehow a death keeps you together, even if you shouldn't be. . . ."

He waits.

She waves a hand outward. "To help remember, is what I think I'm trying to say."

"That's the pain in your poetry?"

"Oh, I don't know," she says. "That's a hard question to answer. And I'm not sure it's pain exactly." She takes a long swallow of champagne. He raises the bottle to fill her glass again, and she lets him.

"What did you mean by 'the shit'?" she asks. "You said in your letter you were trying to 'transcend the shit.'"

"It's not important," he says. "It's just financial stuff. I'm not in particularly good shape at the moment."

"No one is these days."

"I suppose that's true. I didn't like it when you went to England."

"You're funny. You don't even know me."

"I'm not so sure about that. I loved the postcard you sent."

"You'd have loved the pub."

"The forty kinds of malt whiskey. It was your birthday."

"Yes."

"So how old are you now? Forty-six?"

"Yes. When's yours?"

"New Year's Day."

"So you're . . .?"

"Forty-five now."

"Then I'm older than you."

"By two months. An older woman."

"Did we know that then? I wonder. My sister named a goldfish after you. Cal."

"And you think *I'm* funny."

"I guess I talked about you incessantly when I got home from camp. When did you give up the name?"

"Sometime in high school, I think."

She looks out at the water, as if at an apparition there. He looks to see what she is seeing.

"Charles, what happened to us that week?"

"I think it's simple," he says. "We fell in love."

"Is that possible, for two fourteen-year-olds to fall in love?"

"What do you think?"

She looks off to the side, into the woods beyond the clearing, "Where is it? Do you know?"

"I think it must be in there, where you're looking."

"It's strange. For months afterward, possibly even longer, I thought that I would marry you."

"I cried all the way home in the car," he says. "My mother never let me forget it. It was a three-hour car ride. I told you what she said when I told her I'd given you the bracelet."

"I wish I could have found it."

"It probably disintegrated or turned green. I think I paid a dollar and a half for it at the camp store."

"That was a lot then."

He laughs. "I remember that summer I saved up

twenty-four dollars from my paper route and bought a turntable and a bunch of forty-fives."

"The songs you sent. They were from then?"

"Most of them. 'Where or When' was from the summer we met. I played it endlessly."

"The lyrics . . .," she says. She takes a sip of champagne, swallows thoughtfully, as if pondering the words of the song.

"They're extraordinary," he says. "Though what's more extraordinary is how I can possibly have understood them then. I suppose . . ." He looks out over the lake—a flat surface of sterling. "If I played it so often after I met you that summer, which is what I did, I had to have been envisioning a future reunion. In other words, I wasn't experiencing the song as it's meant to be experienced—a man remembering a former love—but rather I was the boy already imagining meeting you again after some time had elapsed. For instance, the line 'The clothes you're wearing are the clothes you wore . . .' I'd have been thinking of finding you one day, and you'd be wearing the thin cotton dress that came just below your knees."

"Or Bermuda shorts."

"Or Bermuda shorts."

" 'It seems we stood and talked like this before . . .' "

He looks at her, adds another line: " 'We looked at each other in the same way then . . .' "

" 'But I can't . . .' " She seems unable to finish.

" '. . . remember where or when,' " he says quietly.

He sits, one leg crossed at the knee, a glass in his hand. He wonders if these are the exact same benches they sat on when they were kids. He shakes his head. He knows he will never understand this. They are, simultaneously, the children they were then and the man and woman they are now. As the water itself, this ancient lake, is the same and yet not. As the trees overhead are the same and yet not. He has never been able fully to comprehend time, now knows it is infinitely more mysterious than he ever imagined.

"There's another line I like," he says after a time. "It's in the original version, but not sung by Dion & The Belmonts. 'Things you do come back to you, As though they knew the way.'"

A flock of geese flap noisily overhead. She bends forward suddenly, her face in her hands.

He puts his hand on her shoulder, tries to pull her up toward him, but she resists.

"What is it?" he asks.

His heart is tight, his chest in a vise.

He is going to lose her, he is thinking. After all these years of not even having her.

"Oh, God," she cries.

"Charles will do."

She sits up quickly, her mouth in a sudden, wide smile. Her eyes are wet.

She looks at him. Her eyes dart from his eyes to his mouth to the top of his hair, as if examining him for the first time. Back to his eyes. She seems to be trying to find him. To read him.

He knows he will not be hard to read, that it must all be there on his face.

He puts his hand at the side of her chin, holds her face steady and kisses her.

Her mouth is soft and large. He can feel her give. A loosening along her spine. He puts his arms around her, pulls her toward him, and she comes, so that her face is against his shoulder, inside his coat.

She inhales deeply into his shirt. "I can smell you," she says with evident surprise. "I remember how you smell."

He kisses the top of her hair. She puts her mouth against the weave of his shirt. She slides her fingers through a gap between the buttons of his shirt, touches the skin there. He wishes she would unbutton his shirt, thinks if she doesn't, he might do it for her. Instead she takes hold of his tie and loops it twice so that it is wound around her hand.

"You're fond of my tie?" he asks.

She laughs lightly.

He puts his hands inside her coat, inside her suit jacket, holding her rib cage, the warmth of her through the silk of her blouse. He kisses her again, finds the inside of her mouth, and feels lost and light-headed, as if he were spinning.

She makes a small sound.

He puts a hand on her chin, tilts her face more sharply toward his. He kisses her again. She slips her face slightly to the side, finds his fingers. She kisses one finger, then another. He slides a finger inside her mouth. She closes her lips around it, holds it, then lets him withdraw it. He does it again, explores her tongue. Then again, and again.

He withdraws his finger. He slides his hand to her breast, feels the breast through the cloth. He unfastens the top button of her blouse, pushes the fabric of her bra aside. He kisses her nipple, licks it with his tongue, astonishing himself with the boldness of this gesture.

She breaks away, as if they had been tussling like schoolboys.

It has not been a minute since he first kissed her. How did they get to this point so quickly?

Her face is flushed, her mouth reddened. Her hair, at one side, has begun to come loose. There is a faint mottling at her throat and on her forehead. Her blouse is open, exposing the top of her left breast.

"Is this a sacrilege?" she asks.

He takes a breath. The question is light, from someone who no longer believes in sacrilege.

"Absolutely not," he says, matching her apostatic tone. "In fact," he adds, going her one better, although he really believes this now, "I think God is going to be pretty annoyed if after bringing us together again—finally, after all these years—we don't do something about it."

She smiles, but she withdraws. He watches as she fastens the top button of her blouse, tucks her hair up under an invisible pin.

"It's so odd that I remembered how you smell," she says. She leans toward him, breathes his chest through his shirt, but before he can seize her, she has moved away. "I love your shirt," she says, laughing. She sits up straight.

He cannot move.

She looks at him, but in her eyes she seems to withdraw even further. She frowns slightly.

"I think I've been frozen," she says, looking away.

She stands up, gathers her coat around her.

He stands up with her, flustered, wanting to keep her there, to tell her that surely now she is becoming unfrozen, but he cannot find the right words, does not want to have misunderstood her. He remembers the empty bottle, the glasses.

He follows her along the path, up across the lawn, and toward the parking lot. He tosses the bottle and the glasses into a bin.

"We haven't eaten," he says, catching up to her.

"I couldn't. Not now."

"No."

"In any event, I have to get home."

He nods.

"You picked a lunch and not a dinner because you had to go home to your wife?"

He doesn't lie. "Yes," he says. "And also I thought it would be easier for you."

They reach her car. She stands at the door, looking in her pocketbook for the keys, a casual gesture, as if she were a client, and he, out of politeness, were walking her to her car. When what he feels is a longing and a regret so achingly deep, he wants to bend over.

When she finds her keys, she turns so that she is facing him. She opens her mouth as if to say goodbye, as if she had so quickly forgotten what they have just done down by the lake.

"I might not be able to do this," she says.

—————————————— Thursday night, 9:40 P.M.

Dear Siân,

I want to pick up the phone. I want my hand held. I want to call you and lie all night with the phone receiver next to me and know that we have an open connection.

I won't call.

I watched you drive out of the parking lot this afternoon, and I felt desolate.

These letters are so volatile now, I do worry about sending them to you. What happened today was not innocent. I would like to say to you that it felt innocent, but I know that's not true.

I want to make love to you and have it stop time.

If I call the literary supplement and tell them you kissed a man who drives a Cadillac, your reputation will be ruined.

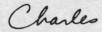

—————————————— Friday, 2 A.M.

Siân,

I have picked up the phone and put it down fifteen times. I want to call you to tell you to meet me later today back at The Ridge. I want to hand deliver this letter.

You said you might not be able to do this. I

want to persuade you that there is nothing more important in life that we have to do now.

I can't sleep. I've been up reading. I dug out one of my old philosophy books and came upon a passage. It's by the French phenomenologist Merleau-Ponty, and it's about sexuality. "Existence permeates sexuality and vice versa," he writes, "so that it is impossible to label a decision or act 'sexual' or 'non-sexual.' There is no outstripping of sexuality any more than there is sexuality enclosed within itself." He also says that no one is saved and no one is totally lost.

I found that last bit reassuring.

I think that I have been somewhat frozen too, but I don't fully understand why.

Your face is as familiar to me as my own.

Just think—it could have been worse: We might have met each other again at sixty-five, not forty-five.

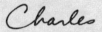

Charles

——————————————————————— Friday, 5 A.M.

Dear Siân,

I am still in my suit. I may never take this shirt off. I am going to frame my tie. I look like hell. I've been listening to "Where or When" all night. About half an hour ago, my wife came down to my study and asked me if I was sick.

You and I have lost thirty-one years. I cannot bear to lose another day.

My study is in ruins. I haven't been able to find your last book of poetry, and I've turned the place upside down looking for it. Now that I've met you—again—I want to read each of the poems—again. I want to know everything there is to know about you.

This house is fucking freezing. I pay $600 a month for heat, and I have to sit here in my overcoat.

I want to kiss your other breast.

I want to believe that this thing that we are doing would have happened—it was just a question of time. My timing in this could not have been worse, and it could not have been better. To meet the woman you were meant to be with is timing that cannot be argued with.

——————————————————— Friday, 11 A.M.

Dear Siân,

I still cannot sleep. I haven't eaten since Wednesday night. I've been drinking Coors Light since I got home from The Ridge, but it hasn't made a dent. I know I should try to lie down, but I have to tell you one more story before I mail these letters off.

I went to the bookstore to buy another copy of

your book of poems. The first copy, I discovered earlier this morning, is on my wife's dresser. I went in to change my shirt, and it was sitting there like a radioactive isotope. Why she should have chosen that book out of all the books in my study to read, I have no idea, but I certainly can't touch it or ask her for it back.

I went to the front desk at the bookstore, and a man and a woman were behind it. I asked the man to find the book for me. The man started to enter the name into the computer, and I said, "I know you have it, or had it, because I bought a copy here several months ago." Then the woman said, "Yeah, it's got a picture of some blond all over the back cover." I said, "Yes, I guess that's the way they market books these days." Then she said back to me, "Yeah, even the academic stuff, they make the women take their blouses off."

I said to her, "She's pretty embarrassed about it herself."

"You know her?" the woman asked.

"She was my girlfriend when I was fourteen," I said.

Charles

HE HAS ALWAYS LIKED WATCHING VOLLEYBALL: THE MOVE-
ments of the players, the high leaps to block shots, a
dozen arms in the air at once, the smash at the net.
They are late, Hadley is already on the court, and the
gym is half filled with parents and siblings who have
rushed an early dinner. He spots Hadley at once in her
blue T-shirt and white shorts, her ponytail whipping behind her as she rises straight off the ground. Charles
follows his wife and two other children to the side of
the gym where there are bleachers. He has not wanted,
for Hadley's sake, to miss this game, but as he quickly
scans the crowd he wishes he could disappear. Whalen
is there, and Costa. Charles has twenty-seven messages
on his machine just from this day alone that he hasn't
returned—though he knows already whom they are
from. Whalen from the bank, who will probably nab
him tonight. GMAC pressing him for a payment on the
Cadillac. The telephone company. Optima. His Citi-

bank Visa. MasterCard. He is fairly certain that Harriet doesn't know yet just how bad their *(his)* financial situation is, an intuition that is borne out when his wife waves at Eddie and Barbara Whalen, sitting downcourt. Charles lifts Anna onto his lap and in doing so catches Muriel Carney's eye. Tom is in the hospital. Has been there since Thanksgiving.

The gym is large, part of a building that was once the town's high school and has now passed on to the middle school. The girls at the center of the blond wooden floor look small and innocent, children still, though they mimic, as Jack does when he plays baseball, the movements of the older athletes they have seen on television or at high school games. Odd, Charles thinks, how many of his peers have girls Hadley's age. Whalen, Costa, Carney. Lidell's Sarah is there too. He cannot make out who is winning, asks the woman beside him for the score. Hadley's team is down two. He can see that his daughter, at the net, is sweating slightly. She is among the tallest of the players on her team, though, he knows, she doesn't have all her growth yet; he guesses she will be close to five ten before she is seventeen.

Hadley leaps, blocks a shot, spikes it straight to the floorboards. The crowd cheers. Charles calls her name. He looks at Harriet, who is smiling broadly, and in doing so he can see that Whalen is making his way along the bleachers, decorously holding his topcoat closed with his hand in the vicinity of his crotch, sliding with apologies past the other parents. Asshole. Whalen will nail him, with Harriet sitting beside him.

There is no escaping this. He feels a twinge of the panic, can feel his blood pressure rising. He stares straight ahead, knowing his face is suffused with color.

"Callahan."

Whalen has perched himself beside Charles, up over his left shoulder. Whalen has soft white skin, thin wisps of hair combed across a bald pate. Charles, glancing quickly at Whalen, makes a silent promise to himself to go bald without attempts at camouflage.

"Eddie."

"Called you all last week. Today."

"I know."

Charles looks over at Harriet, who returns his glance and frowns slightly. She seems surprised to see Whalen sitting behind Charles.

"I don't have the money," Charles says, turning away from Harriet toward Whalen.

"You've missed three months."

"I know that."

"We can't carry this mortgage forever, Charles. If you could just give us some indication of when . . ."

Charles is silent. He hates Whalen's whine. It comes through even on the telephone. Charles knows he cannot pull out of this but doesn't want to have to admit it to Whalen, not right now, not in front of Harriet.

"I'd like to cut you some slack, Callahan," Whalen says, the whine rising a notch. "You know that. But times are tight right now. We're down to the bone ourselves."

Charles removes Anna from his lap. He shifts

slightly on the bench so that only Whalen can hear what he is saying.

"Listen, asshole," he says slowly and deliberately, punctuating *asshole,* knowing as he does so that he is sealing his fate. "I'm watching a fucking volleyball game in which my daughter and your daughter are playing, and I'm sitting here with my wife and two other kids, and I'm not going to fucking discuss my fucking mortgage right now. Is that clear?"

He looks at Whalen long enough to see the man's face turn the color of his shirt, a grayish white. He watches Whalen open his mouth and close it. Charles swivels back to the game, a din ringing in his ears. It's his blood pressure, and his right hand is balled into a fist. Behind him he can hear Whalen stand abruptly. On the court, Hadley is serving. She faults twice, forfeits the serve. Charles winces inwardly for his daughter.

There was no letter today. He went to the post office two, three times. He has calculated that the earliest a letter could have arrived from her would have been today, though she'd have to have written it and mailed it almost immediately upon returning home from The Ridge on Thursday, which seems highly unlikely. He's not sure she could have made it home before five o'clock, the hour the post office closes. He doesn't even know if she will write him now, if he will ever see her again. He sent his own packet of letters to her on Saturday morning, calculating that they would arrive tomorrow. It's entirely possible that she will not respond, will refuse to meet with him. She said at the car that she might not be able to do this. . . .

He lets his eyes wander to the court. He has no idea who is winning. Did Hadley's lost serve cancel out the gain of the blocked shot? He could ask Harriet but does not want to speak to her just now. She might ask him about Whalen. There are several good players on the other team, he can see, focusing on them for the first time. The visitors are wearing black shirts, red shorts. There's a small girl from the other side with a surprisingly powerful serve; no one from Hadley's team can return it. Costa's daughter makes a valiant try, misses. He sees then another girl, a girl from the visiting side who is at least Hadley's height, a girl with dark blond hair pulled into a knot at the back of her head. She's standing in the back row, waiting for the serve. She glances down at her feet, puts her hands together briefly, poised for the shot. A coach calls for a time-out; the girl relaxes her posture. She brings her hand up to the back of her neck, idly touches her hair. She does not have the obvious stance of an athlete, but her pose is graceful, self-contained. The players wait while Costa's daughter reties a shoelace. The tall girl from the visiting side is sweating slightly, on her upper lip, at her temples. She glances up at Charles, across the court, as if she knew that he was watching her.

He might be hallucinating. He *is* hallucinating, he decides. The girls move, the game resumes, but he sees only Siân, a central presence in a swirling collage of outstretched arms and small thin bodies leaping from the shiny wooden floor. He feels light-headed, dizzy, but he is certain he is watching Siân. He knows the hallucination is a product of his unraveling. He hasn't eaten or slept in days. And yet the vision seems also to be a gift, a peering into a past that has been denied to him. He watches the girl arc her body off the ground and knows that it is Siân he sees. He aches sharply for the loss of her, feels his eyes fill suddenly, as if he'd been stung. He glances quickly at his wife, realizes that Harriet has been staring at him. He looks back at the game. The hallucination fades as quickly as it came to him. He wonders then: Was he seeing Siân as she really was, or as he imagines her to be?

He feels a hand on his knee, looks down. It is Harriet's, reaching across Jack and Anna, their children.

"Charles," she says.

In bed that night, when his wife reaches for him, he knows that this time he cannot refuse her. It is not exactly a challenge—he and Harriet do not engage each other in that way—yet he knows that in the gesture there is a question. He lets her touch him, prays that his body will respond, but in the darkness, even with his eyes shut, he sees only other faces, other images, that distract him. Siân as a young girl, Siân's face by the lake, her breast exposed to him. The images are not sexual; they make him want to cry. He is afraid he will cry, thinks instead of Whalen's whine. His body is hopelessly limp, unresponsive. He does not want to hurt his wife.

"I want you to come first," he whispers, shifting his

body quickly, putting his hand to her, hoping she will allow this, will accept this, will let his own failure go.

She puts her hand on his hand, makes him stop.

"I'm just exhausted," he says feebly.

She takes his hand away from her body, rolls over with her back to him.

He is at the post office before eight, the Cadillac humming, waiting for Harry Noonan to arrive and open the front door to the postboxes. This morning, Charles was out of bed before Harriet, so as to avoid a reprise of the previous night. He showered, shaved, dressed, drank some coffee, and sat in his office, trying ineffectually to clear the debris off his desk while he listened to the early morning sounds of his wife and children in other rooms. He thinks briefly of his outburst with Whalen at the gym last night, nervously taps the steering wheel as a familiar knot forms in his stomach. It was not smart, he knows, to have let his anger boil to the surface. The bank will foreclose, he is certain of this now, but with children in the house, they'll have to give him at least sixty days to find another place to live. Harriet and the kids will have Christmas in the house, and it's conceivable he may not even have to tell Harriet until the new year.

Christmas. New Year's Eve.

She has said she may not be able to see him again. There may, at this very moment, be a letter inside the post office repeating that intention. Or worse (or perhaps not worse), there may be no letter at all.

Four past eight, Harry Noonan finally drives up in

his gray Isuzu Trooper. Charles nods through the windshield at Noonan, waits for Harry to unlock the front door before getting out of his car. Charles's early arrival at the post office is not unprecedented—he often begins his day by getting the mail—but he does not want to appear particularly overeager today. After a minute or two, however, he follows Noonan through the lobby with the postboxes—the mail won't be in them yet—and into the main room, where Noonan is already sorting through a large stack of envelopes, his parka still on.

"Callahan."

"Harry."

"You heard anything this morning about the storm we're supposed to get?"

"No. It'll probably just be rain. Freezing rain. Screw up the roads."

"Probably so."

Noonan sets aside a small pile of familiar-looking envelopes—one from the phone company, others from Citibank, the cable company, the bank (The Bank)—and one large unfamiliar manila envelope. No blue envelopes, but Charles focuses on the manila envelope, reaches for it. The handwriting is hers; there is no return address. His hand begins at once to shake; he feels his chest constrict. He tucks the envelope under his arm, puts his hands, to still them, into the pockets of his overcoat. He wants to get back to the safety of his car, tear open the gummed seal.

"Thanks, Harry," he says, turning to leave.

"Callahan."

Charles looks back at Noonan, who is studying Charles over the rims of his half-glasses.

"You forgot your mail."

Charles holds the envelope in the car, taps it twice against the steering wheel. He feels as he used to as a kid, opening his report card or an admissions letter from college—pausing on the brink of relief or disaster, mumbling incoherent prayers. He takes a deep breath, exhales. He slits open the seal. Inside are three blue envelopes, marked "1," "2," and "3." He opens the first envelope, quickly scans the letter, devours it like a junkie. His eyes fill; he blinks. A strangled, muted sound—something between a sob and a sigh—escapes him. He cannot read the other letters here. He lays the opened letter and the two unopened letters on the passenger seat, puts the key into the ignition, and, nearly blind, backs out of the parking lot. A sharp, stinging rain begins on the windshield. He drives to the bridge and the beach.

Dear Charles,

I will write this letter. My hand has been poised
over the paper for fifteen minutes—the equivalent
of a kind of speechlessness that comes from having
too much to say and not being able to find the right
words with which to say it.

It is easier to sit on a wooden bench or to listen
to imagined music than to explain why I can think
of little else and why, walking across the lawn to the
parking lot, I felt different to myself. It is possible
that today I have begun to become unfrozen. That
would seem to be a good in itself, yet I wonder what
it will do to myself and to my family.

I found your presence reassuring, your body and
your voice familiar to me, as I seem to have been
to you. How that can be so, I cannot say. The two
of us together, down by the lake—it seemed that we
were both reality and metaphor at once for
something I barely understand.

My fantasies are simple ones and are products of
what I think is a kind of emotional exhaustion—the
result of trying to hold myself and my family
together all these years. I dream of having my hand
held. I don't really dream of sexual passion. That, this
afternoon, was unexpected.

You did not ask about my husband, though I
asked about your wife. I tried at lunch to convey
something of my marriage, but I suspect I did it badly.
When I met Stephen in graduate school, I mistook

141

*his silence for a kind of appealing reserve. I didn't
know then that I had met him during the two
happiest years of his life, when he was as far from
the farm as he had ever been.*

*He is wedded to the farm, even more than to me,
but he has never really been happy here. It is, for
him, his own peculiar kind of destiny.*

I feel extremely disloyal writing even this much.

I must go to bed now, but I doubt that I will sleep.

*I imagine us meeting intermittently over a period
of many years—possibly even into old age—a thread
running through our lives.*

*When I move a certain way, I can smell you on
my skin.*

———————————————————— Friday, 9:20 A.M.

Charles,

    *I'm glad I wrote that letter to you, and I will
send it along with this one, but in the early
morning light of family and a child and a house and
a life, I know this is not going to be possible. I think
somehow, somewhere, you know this too. There is,
probably, a great affinity between us—perhaps that's
what drew us together as children and again yesterday.
But I know this is not going to be manageable. There
must be, on your part, some relief in reading these
words.*

It was tantalizing for me, the vision I had of how this might work. But did I really imagine I could see you from time to time and then forget about you and go on with my life in the intervals?

I know that you understand that what happened yesterday was not casual, that it was, potentially, the first step of a thousand steps, and that ending it now is essential. What happened between us on that bench, for those few brief moments, was dangerous.

Yesterday, driving home from The Ridge, I felt deliciously female and wanted, as though I were carrying around inside me a wonderful secret.

I did not sleep all night.

I do not want you to do anything to hurt your wife or your family.

Siân

——————————————————————— Friday, 6:45 P.M.

Charles,

You will think me deranged, or descending into madness.

I wrote the letter to you this morning, then I took my daughter to the playground. It was very quiet and peaceful there—it's really too late in the season to go to the playground, but Lily was bundled up and warm. She went immediately to a small sandbox, and I was grateful for the opportunity to sit on a bench and think.

All I can think about is you.

You held my shoulder in the restaurant. And then you held my hand, and I turned my head away, and you asked if it upset me, and I said no, when what I really wanted to say was, "I can't breathe."

And then I thought, sitting on the bench, with my daughter playing in the sandbox: This is madness. I just wrote this man a letter telling him it couldn't happen, when all I want—all I want—is for him to make love to me.

I am walking around in a feverish state. I am not sleeping not eating.

I know it would be better for everyone if we didn't see each other ever again.

I want you to know that I take at least equal responsibility for what happens now.

I ask myself all the time, every minute, every hour: What is this?

Siân

❦ ❦ ❦ ❦ ❦ ❦

HIS HANDS ARE SO WET AND FROZEN HE CAN BARELY MAKE
the phone work. He's forgotten his glasses and cannot
see the digits, taps the numbers in as if working braille.
The phone is exposed, an outdoor box at the side of the
Qwik Stop. He hopes no one he knows will pass by:
What's Callahan doing at a pay phone in this filthy
weather, with his own house not two miles away? Needles of frozen rain sting the back of his neck. He turns
his collar up, wishes he had an umbrella. The sleet
drips off his nose.

"Hello?"

It is a woman's voice; it is Siân's. But her voice
sounds tentative, as if she had not wanted to answer
the phone.

"Siân?"

There is a silence. A long silence.

"This is—"

"I know who it is," she says slowly. He hears a small

sound, a tiny sound from the back of her throat. "Oh, God . . . ," she says.

"Charles will—"

"I know. I know." Her voice is strained. He thinks she may be crying, but he can't tell without seeing her. "I thought when I said I might not be able to do this I'd never hear from you again," she says in a rush.

"You had to have known that I would call," he says. "Did you get my letters yet?"

"No."

"You'll get them today. I just got yours."

There is a silence at her end, though he thinks he can hear her breathing.

"Siân?"

"Yes?"

"We have to meet again. You know that."

"Yes."

"I want to meet you today, now."

"I can't—"

"No, not today. The weather is awful. Is it snowing there?"

"Freezing rain."

"Same here. Tomorrow?"

"Tomorrow?"

"I don't want to wait. I won't wait. I have to do this."

"I'll try."

"Same place?"

"All right."

"But earlier. Can you get there by ten?"

She seems to be thinking, calculating. "Yes," she says hesitantly. "I think so."

"Good." He lets out his breath. "Siân?"

"Yes?"

"I know you'll think I'm crazy, but I want you to know, in case something happens to me and I don't get there, that I love you."

The silence at her end is so long, he thinks she may have hung up. He wishes he could see her face.

"And there's something else," he says.

"What?" Her voice is quiet.

"I don't know how I know this on the basis of only one meeting," he says, "but I'm sure of this. . . ."

"What?"

"I know I always have."

He is standing at the side of his car when she drives into the parking lot. Ten past ten. The day is frosty and translucent; the storm from yesterday blew the front through, leaving in its wake a sky so blue it looks almost neon. She emerges from the car, slings her pocketbook over her shoulder, shuts the door. He watches as she crosses the parking lot to the Cadillac. They stand facing each other for an instant, and then he embraces her, folds her into him. She comes willingly, as if she, too, has been anticipating this moment for days. He can feel her trembling, and she says so: "I'm shaking," she says, as if embarrassed. "I'm just shaking."

He holds her at arm's length, looks at her face, kisses her. Her mouth opens; he feels as if he is pouring himself into her.

He breaks away. "I've got a room," he says.

She composes herself then. He thinks for a moment

that she may protest, may not be ready for a room yet and what that implies, but she says nothing, seems to be waiting for him to lead the way. He takes her hand, walks with her across the parking lot, up the steps of the inn and into the lobby. Again she is wearing black—a black coat, black high heels—and he senses, rather than sees, the slight limp as she walks. Inside the lobby, he turns to her and says quietly, "This is the hard part, walking past the front desk. I've already checked us in."

"I don't feel guilty," she says. "It's all right."

He cannot remember the last time he booked a room in a clandestine manner with a woman. Certainly not since he has been married. He has been faithful to Harriet throughout their marriage, as he imagines she has been to him. Yet it is not guilt he feels so much as awkwardness—as if he were a young man who has had little experience with women. He wonders, too, not for the first time, if it will work—if, in the throes of an emotion he can barely define, he will be able to make love to Siân Richards. He has tried, over the past several days, to envision making love to her, but he has not been able to bring these fantasies into clear focus. He can only remember them as children. He would like to say to her that the room is simply for convenience, for privacy, so that they can talk out of earshot of others, get to know each other again, but he knows that would sound disingenuous. She walks slightly ahead of him, to his right. He gives directions behind her. The room is on the top floor, on the west wing. The wing in which the boys once had their rooms. The view from the room is out to the back, to the lake. He has already been to the room, inspected it.

He puts the key into the lock, opens the door, and lets her pass through. In the center of the room is an austere four-poster, the bed covered with a white du-vet. The other furniture in the room—a tall dresser that conceals a television, a washstand on which there is a white porcelain bowl and pitcher, two silk-upholstered chairs—is of matching cherry, either authentically eigh-teenth century or intended to resemble that era. Enter-ing the room again, he marvels at the transformation. When he was a boy here, the rooms contained two sets of bunk beds, four crates intended as storage cabinets.

Siân stands with her hands in the pockets of her coat, walks to the window to see the view. He joins her at the window, puts a hand on her shoulder, looks out with her. The sun glints harshly off the water. He makes a gesture so as to remove her coat; she lets the coat and her pocketbook slide off. She is wearing a black dress with a gray jacket. Again she has worn her hair up, twisted into a knot held with a clip.

He bends down, puts his lips to the nape of her neck. She seems to shiver. She lets her head fall slightly forward.

"You remembered," she says, her voice barely a whis-per.

"Of course I remembered," he says.

He turns her to him, walks with her the two or three steps to the bed. She sits at its edge, he beside her.

She opens her palms. "I'm not . . ."

She looks at him, a question on her face. She opens

her mouth as if to finish her sentence, but he kisses
her, brings her with him onto the bed. Her mouth is
open, welcoming, but he feels, too, as if at any minute
she might pull away. He puts his hand under the skirt
of her dress, feels the skin of her hip, her belly. Her
stockings stop at the top of her thigh. He raises her
skirt so that he can see her body.

She has on a short black slip, the lace falling across
her abdomen. She lets him remove her underwear. He
finds her then, slips one finger inside, then another.
He moves his fingers back and forth slowly, savoring
her. He bends toward her, his fingers still lost inside
her, and lets his mouth hover over hers. She opens her
mouth slightly, as if to receive him; he can see her
teeth, her tongue. He opens his mouth but does not
kiss her yet. Their mouths are not an inch apart. She
lifts herself slightly toward him, waiting for him. He
can feel her breath on his lips. He removes his fingers
from inside her, puts them to her mouth. He traces
the outline of her bottom lip. She reaches for his
hand, pulls his fingers toward her, into her mouth,
lets him move them slowly back and forth there as he
did inside her.

Quickly he unfastens his belt buckle, enters her. He
raises himself up on his hands; he has to be able to see
her face. She watches him, closes her legs around him.
He can feel the cool smoothness of her legs on the
backs of his. She watches him steadily, closes her eyes
briefly, intently, only at the end. He is not far behind
her, and he knows, when he comes, knows it for a cer-

tainty, that he will never want to make love to any other woman but Siân Richards again.

After a time, under him, she turns her face to the side. He raises himself up so that he can see her. She is smiling.

"What is it?" he asks, beginning to smile himself.

She shakes her head slowly. She turns back to him, gazes at him steadily, seeing him as he knows he has never been seen before—not by Harriet, not by any other woman. Her smile is full of knowledge, beyond the circumstances of just this day, just this bed.

"I've been waiting for you," she says.

She is sitting on the edge of the bed in her black slip. She has removed her jacket, her dress. Her hair has fallen down to one side, barely held with the clip. He is nearly naked, under the covers, propped up against the pillows. He likes watching her move in her slip.

"Do you always wear black?" he asks her.

She shrugs, crosses her legs. "I suppose so. It's easier that way. Everything goes with everything."

"I think I'm going to kill every man who's ever heard you have an orgasm," he says.

"There haven't been many," she says. "And in any event, if we keep this up, we'll soon surpass our marriages."

They have made love three or four times. He is no longer sure how to define the act of making love, or how to count the experiences, each time somehow merging into another, exciting another. They haven't even had lunch yet.

"Well, it's not going to take *me* long," he says.

She laughs. "That's a sweet thing to say."

"It's true."

"It's odd," she says, "how the fourteen-year-olds really didn't know what was happening to them, and now the forty-six-year-olds don't really know what is happening to them either."

"One of us is only forty-five."

She raps him on his arm. He flinches in mock pain.

"*I* can't define this," he says. "I can only relate it to how I felt about you at fourteen."

He sits up, lifts her hair, kisses her again at the nape of the neck. "When I do this now," he says, "I smell a sexual odor. It's something about my breath on your neck." He pulls back, looks at her neck. "You have a stork bite," he says.

"A what?"

"A stork bite. At least that's what it looks like. A birthmark. It's just inside your hairline."

She touches the back of her neck. She stands up, walks to the window, looks out at the lake. He gets out of bed, stands beside her. He is wearing only his shirt, unbuttoned.

"That was very strange," he says, "when we sat down there last week, looking out at the water."

"What did it mean to you?"

"I don't know," he says. "It seemed like John the Baptist himself was going to emerge right then from the lake."

"That's not a very Catholic image."

"No."

"Where's it coming from?"

"I suppose I just wanted to jump in and be cleansed. I didn't want to have to imagine you with anyone else."

She puts her hand on his shoulder, slides her hand down his back.

"I think this was supposed to happen," she says.

"Can we trust that?" he asks.

She is silent for a moment. "I think if you can't trust this, you can't trust the universe."

The room, his chest, expand. He wants to open the window, call out to the waiters.

"I think we were meant to have mated," she adds.

He smiles. He loves the word "mated." It suggests to him something primitive, simple, animal-like, beyond thought, or before thought, like the way she has recognized his scent.

"Yes," he says. "I believe that."

"And I've never even seen your children."

"Nor I yours."

"We won't ever have children together," she says. "Well, we probably won't have children together. What I mean is, we ought not to have children together."

A new thought enters his mind. He is appalled that he has not been concerned about this earlier—more appalled by his next thought: While he is worried that they have made love unprotected, he wishes fervently that he could make her pregnant.

"I ought to have mentioned this sooner," he says, "but . . ."

She shakes her head quickly. "No. I didn't bring anything. But I'm not sure it's an issue for me anymore."

He is not altogether certain what she means by this, but he lets her statement go. "We have enough children," he says.

"We've only known each other six days."

"Six days and one week."

"Six days, one week, and thirty-one years," she says.

He folds her into him, brings her head into his shoulder. She has asked him in a letter, "What *is* this?" The question of meaning, he knows, might not be able to be answered. Is this relationship, he wonders, regressive or progressive? Are they each merely trying to recapture an immature childhood love? Or is this a chance—the chance of a lifetime—to have a rich, mature, sexual love with the person you were meant to be with? Odd how these very questions are implicit in the song he has found again and now likes so much. *Things you do come back to you, as though they knew the way.*

She touches the cloth of his shirt, brings it to her face, inhales deeply.

"I love the smell of you," she says.

She has put herself together as best she can, has redone her hair, though she had no makeup with her to cover the faint mottling at her forehead. Her gray jacket is wrinkled. "Next time," she said in the room, his heart lifting at the words, "I'll have to bring some things with me so that I can shower, fix myself before lunch."

They are sitting at the same banquette they had before. The room is much as it was last week, except that sheer white curtains have been drawn across the large floor-to-ceiling windows to protect the diners from the trapezoidal blocks of bright sunlight that fall at this hour across the dining room. He has had a vodka, she a glass of wine; he, oysters; she, salmon. Surprisingly—or perhaps not surprisingly—he was hungry for the first time in weeks. He feels exhausted but exhilarated. She sits slightly turned toward him, her knee just touching his thigh. He has his hand on her leg, on the skirt of her dress. Though she is not precisely smiling, her face gives off a glow as if she were.

"You're beautiful," he says. He knows that she does not have an unflawed body, as he does not; and he knows that she is forty-six, not twenty-six. And yet he cannot, at this moment, conceive of another woman being more appealing to him than she.

"*You're* beautiful," she says.

"I don't think anyone's ever said that to me before."

She puts her hand on his knee, touches him lightly there. "I've never done this," she says. "I mean I've never been unfaithful."

"Nor have I."

"I don't have what you would call a very bad marriage," she says slowly, removing her hand. "But Stephen and I are not close. We don't . . . We hardly ever . . ." She makes a gesture as if to include the experiences they have just had together in the room in the west wing.

He puts a hand up quickly. "Don't," he says. "I can't. Not yet."

She looks down at the table.

"We have to be careful," he says.

She agrees quickly. "I don't want your wife to be hurt."

"No. I didn't mean that. I mean we have to be careful with each other."

She studies him. "I sometimes think about the next thirty-one years," she says.

"So do I."

"I wonder, how much time do we have left? The second half? The third third? And it's all so serendipitous. If you hadn't bought the Sunday paper that morning, we wouldn't be here now."

"Does it matter, the number of years?" he asks. He can hear the sudden heat in his voice. "Isn't it worth it even to have one year, one month? Isn't that just as valuable—or is it really the accumulation of hours?"

She sits silently. He knows she cannot answer this question. She reaches into her pocketbook. "I brought some pictures," she says. "To give you an idea of the years in between. And I wanted to show you my daughter."

He takes the small, neat pile of photographs from her hand, puts on his glasses.

"That's me in high school," she says, pointing to a picture of a girl in a pageboy haircut, a simple sweater and pearls. She is not wearing glasses in this picture, and he is struck by how much older than a girl she looks. She has to have been only sixteen, seventeen at best. Yet her eyes have an ageless quality—a gravity that belies her youth. "And that's me in Senegal." He looks at a photograph of a tall, thin, angular woman in dark glasses with a colored cloth wrapped around her breasts, forming a dress. "It's all the women wore there," she explains. There are other people in the photograph as well, but no men. She shows him other pictures—some of a small, pretty child with long blond hair. None of her husband.

He stops suddenly at one photograph, can go no further. It's of Siân and a baby. She looks to be in her late twenties or early thirties, and she's cradling the baby in her arms, as if she were nursing the infant. This has to be the son who died.

He puts the packet of photographs in his lap, looks across at the far wall.

"It hurts that this is you, and I wasn't there," he says.

He hands the photographs back to her. He can feel the pressure of the minutes left to them. He glances surreptitiously at his watch, but she sees him.

"What time is it?" she asks.

"I don't want to tell you," he says.

"I'll have to know," she says.

"I was hoping we could go back to the room, but I know you can't."

"We'll come back here."

"When?"

"I'm not sure. It'll be hard to get away."

"But we have to."

"Yes."

"Can I call you?"

She looks down at her hands. She raises her head, sighs. "He's almost never in the house between four and five," she says. "But I have Lily then. It won't be easy."

As he pays the bill, she gathers her coat around her. They leave the dining room. He puts his hands in the pockets of his pants, hunches his shoulders against the cold. He's left his overcoat back in the room, will have to retrieve it when she has left. They walk together across the parking lot to her car, the small black Volkswagen.

"If we think about what might have been," she says, taking his arm, "we'll drive ourselves mad."

They reach her car. She puts the key in the lock. She looks up at him. He is aware only that within seconds she will leave him.

"Will we be allowed to do this?" she asks.

"I can't conceive of not doing this," he says, answering her.

He puts his arms around her, brings her head into his shoulder. As he does so, a car pulls into the parking lot. The driver, making the turn, is an older woman with short, graying hair, a waitress perhaps, or a chef in the kitchen. The woman looks at him, smiles broadly, gives him a thumbs-up sign. He smiles back at her.

"This is it," he says to Siân.

Minutes later, entering the room to retrieve his coat, he sees the bed, still unmade, still rumpled. He sits at the edge of the bed, notices a stain on the bottom sheet. He touches the stain with his fingers, closes his eyes. How can they be apart, he wonders, with this evidence of their union?

The girl knew, on the second day, that the boy would speak to her. All the afternoon before—inside the rooms of the old mansion and out on the lawns, and even by the pool when finally they had been allowed a swim—she knew that he was watching her. He wore red bathing trunks and dove with his body pointed like a knife, and when he came up, his hair, though short, was flattened, and he was looking at her.

On the second day, just before noon, she left the art room, where the others were, and walked along the path to the lake. Such a walk was not on the schedule, but it was not forbidden either. She was not a recluse necessarily, though she did often prefer to be alone.

Walking from the wide lawn into the thicket of trees was, she thought, like entering a cathedral where the walls were made of tall pines rather than the large hand-cut stones of the Catholic church near her home. The breeze from the lake drifted up the path through the trees, and the walk was dark, in shadow, sheltered from the glare of the midday sun. She made her way with her hands in her pockets, and when she heard the footfalls behind her, she kept her pace steady, did not hesitate or turn around. She entered the clearing, walked along the aisle between the wooden benches, sat at the one closest to the water. In front of her was the cross, and beyond that, the surface of the lake stretched to the other shore. Her being at this camp, she knew, was not about the cross. She understood already, even at fourteen, that the cross was historical, that it was but one of several ways the adults around her had seized upon to define hope, though she liked the discipline and the ritual of her church, the cadence of the Latin words.

He sat on a bench not far from hers, facing toward the water as she was. He said Hi in a shy voice, glancing at her sideways, and she said Hi too, looking at him quickly. He told her his name, and she said hers, though each knew the other's already. He asked her where she was from, and she asked him where he was from, and they gave their answers casually, not knowing that these answers sealed their fate. He seemed like her, she thought, not withdrawn, but someone comfortable with his own company. He said he'd left the room where the others were because he already had a wallet and couldn't see the sense of making another, not one held together with gimp anyway. She nodded and smiled. She said she wasn't much for crafts herself. She preferred other activities—the swimming and the archery, badminton. He said, smiling at his own cockiness, tempting fate, that he was pretty good at badminton and that they ought to play sometime. She said then, matching his self-mocking tone, that she was all right herself, and she might, if he was lucky, give him a game. They sat silently then, looking out at the water, both with smiles still left on their faces, until the smiles, after a time, faded.

He stood up, moved over to her bench. He sat beside her. He held a stick, etched figures in the dirt beneath their feet. They talked of their families and their schools, their new counselors, the routine at camp, each knowing that the casual questions and answers masked another dialogue, one spoken with averted eyes, small gestures. She crossed her legs; he scratched his arm.

The lake was not for swimming. At the shoreline, the bottom turned dark with roots and weeds. There were fish in the lake, and sitting there, even under the hot sun, they could sometimes see the movement of a bass or a perch at the surface. A bell rang a melody, tolled twelve chimes, signaling lunch. They could not be away for this event, would be looked for, spoken to. She thought she might not mind that, except that then the others would know they had been found together and would be watching them.

She stood first and said they would have to go up the path now to the dining room. He flung the stick into the water. She watched it sail and fall. It was understood already, even on this first meeting, that they must return separately, and so he said, chivalrously, that he just wanted to inspect the boathouse before going back—allowing her to walk up the lawn first, accepting for himself the greater risk.

She hesitated, then acquiesced. She knew he saw her hesitation, that he knew she did not want to leave the clearing, this tentative beginning. He put his hands in his pockets, made markings in the soft dry dirt with the toe of his sneaker. Beyond them up the hill, they could hear the slap of a screen door, the muffled chatter of the others.

This afternoon, he said, and she nodded.

When we were children, you held my hand. And later, when we lay together on the damp, rumpled sheet, when I said, This is overtaking us, you said to me, This is only holding your hand.

The summer that I met you I began to bleed. The winter that I met you again, I stopped. I used to think that that was what we had missed together—my womanhood.

At the room at the inn, the room that used to be a dormitory room, you slid your fingers inside me, and I thought to myself: This is as intimate as I have ever been.

At the room at the inn, I lay under you. Your face was over mine. I looked up at you, at your mouth and at your eyes, and I thought: I know this man. It was the shock of recognition.

I brought pictures to the inn, to show you who I'd been, but I saw at once my mistake, the hurt in your eyes, and you said, It hurts that I wasn't with you.

You sat in a chair in the room. I sat astride you and

looked at your face. You were wearing a blue-striped shirt, a red tie loosened at the collar. I looked at the outline of your face, the elegant jaw, the brown eyes, the mouth, the straight lower lip, and I saw the boy who had left me, the young man I had never known.

I watched you sit at the edge of the bed and bend to put your shoes on. I was standing behind you, and you didn't know I was watching. I saw the curve of your long back, the vulnerability of that long back, and I thought: I will always love this man.

I wanted to ask you questions, but could not. Did you know when you made your babies? Did you kiss your wife when she was in labor? When did you tell your wife that you loved her? Did you think your wife was beautiful?

And now I wonder this: To what extent does time distort memory?

him with apologies past due and other parents. Assholes. Whalen will nail him, with Harriet sitting beside him.

HE IS AWARE, AS HE STANDS IN LINE, THAT HE IS AN OB-
ject of scrutiny. He is not certain, however, if the cause
is his unshaven appearance or if it stems from something else altogether—a demeanor that is both distracted and focused, is lost and yet edgy. He has been
up all night writing letters, four of which he now holds
inside a large manila envelope. He slept only two
hours, after the kids left the house this morning, on the
couch in his clothes. Since returning home from The
Ridge, he has been unable to enter his and Harriet's
bedroom, to look at the marriage bed, as if to do so
were a kind of double betrayal—both to his wife and to
the woman he made love to yesterday.

He feels trapped, third in line, at least seven people
behind him. Possibly, he thinks, the reason everyone is
staring at him is that they know he has lost his office,
will almost certainly lose his house soon. Another recession casualty. Even Harriet has lately been attribut-

ing his bizarre behavior to his financial difficulties—an attribution that makes him feel both relieved and guilty. She no longer even asks why he doesn't come to bed, why he doesn't eat, as if she had decided to let this minor breakdown take its course.

He has come to the post office at the worst imaginable time, twelve-fifteen, lunch hour, and in the pre-Christmas rush too. He thinks of leaving, returning later, but he knows he must get these letters out of the house, get them off to Siân. Moving up to second in line, he reaches to the counter, snags an Express Mail address label, finds his pen in a jacket pocket. He thinks, as he has done all morning, of what they were doing at precisely this hour yesterday, reliving the day in fifteen-minute intervals. At twelve-fifteen, he recalls, they were still in bed, hadn't gone down to lunch yet. His mind swims with erotic images. Today he will call her at four. He needs to hear her voice.

The elderly woman in front of him puts her purse on the counter, removes her wallet, and painstakingly counts, in coins and bills, the cost of her transactions. Even Noonan, normally stoic, looks impatiently at his watch and then at the long line that has opened the door, letting in the cold, and sighs.

"Callahan," he says, nodding slowly over the woman's head.

"Harry," Charles says.

"Cold out there."

"Bitter."

"Whatya got there?"

"Express," Charles says.

The woman in front of Charles moves away. Charles puts his packet on the counter. He wonders what Noonan will think about the address. The second time this week—an address he's been writing to all fall. Noonan looks at the package, weighs it, begins to attach the Express Mail label Charles has filled out.

The idea comes to him then. He looks at the long line of people behind him, glances at Noonan across the counter. Noonan has just indicated an amount of money, is waiting for Charles to pay.

No one will understand this, he knows. But she will. *She* will.

"Hold it a minute there, Harry."

Charles strips off his topcoat, then his suit jacket underneath, lays these garments on the counter. He loosens his tie, slips it through his collar. He unbuttons the front of his shirt, then the cuffs. He takes the shirt off, folds it into as compact a bundle as he can manage. He reaches across the counter, stuffs the shirt inside the packet with the letters, seals it again, slides the packet back to Noonan. Noonan looks at Charles. Charles puts his jacket and his topcoat back on. slips the tie into a pocket. He buttons the overcoat all the way up to the collar. He takes out his wallet.

"What do I owe you now?" he asks Harry Noonan.

Four

The air was soft and moist, the early morning air of a day that later would be hot but now was cool from a breeze off the water. She liked best, she thought, the way the pink light filtered through the leaves and highlighted the foliage along the banks. It was the third day or the fourth, and they had found a way each day to be together. He had said the night before to meet him early, at the boathouse.

He was there already. She could see him through the wide entrance, a white shirt in the shadows, bending to a boat, wrestling with a line. She walked beneath the wooden canopy to the dock. When they arranged to be together, neither ever said, We shouldn't be here, or, We might get caught. She had left her room before the others had awakened.

He rowed from the center of the boat, while she sat in the stern. She liked the smooth rotation of his arms as he pulled the oars, though sometimes, in his haste, the oars slapped the water, spraying them. Once, when he shifted in his seat, their knees touched, his through the cotton of his slacks, hers bare. He looked up at her quickly then, glanced away. He rowed to the middle of the lake, then let them drift out of sight toward the westward shore. He banked the oars in the boat and rested.

A sweat had broken out already around his neck and on his forehead. He took off his shoes and socks. He handed her his watch, and when he dove into the water, she thought later that he had done it as much to break the tension as to cool himself. He came up laughing and told her that if he drowned, she should give the watch to his little brother. She smiled. She wished that she could dive in with him, but she knew that they could not both go back with wet clothes, and besides, she reasoned, they couldn't abandon the boat, not without a line or a mooring.

He swam away, then back again. He swam on his side, then cut the water with a crawl. The water around them was dark in the early morning light, though away from them, the surface had a pink shimmer.

He returned to the boat, circled it on his back. He looked happy; his swimming seemed effortless. He spouted water like a whale, enjoyed showing off. He asked her questions, questions that were easier to ask from the water: Had she ever done anything really bad? Did she have a boyfriend at home? And she answered him. She did not have a boyfriend, she said, and once she had hitched a ride on the highway with a truckdriver.

What happened? he asked her, hanging on to the side of the boat with one hand.

He drove me to the next town.

Then what? he asked.

She was sorry now that she had chosen this story to tell.

He tried to kiss me, she said.

The word hung between them, a charged word at fourteen, a word that lay at the center of their thoughts. He looked stricken, would not ask the next question, though she knew she had to answer it.

I didn't let him, she said. I ran away from the truck, walked all the way home.

How long? he asked.

Five miles.

He flung himself back into the water, sank down as if with relief, bobbed up again.

That's not something bad that *you* did, he said.

Sure it is, she said. I got into the truck, didn't I?

He seemed to think about this. Well, that was stupid, but it wasn't bad, he said.

I thought it was bad, she said.

Did you tell your parents? he asked.

Of course not, she said.

I'll bet you told it at confession, he said. I'll bet you thought it was a sin.

He grabbed hold of the side of the boat, hoisted himself in. His shirt was a translucent peach, stuck to his skin. His pants were molded to the contours of his body. She looked away.

She was slightly irritated: She *had* thought it was a sin. Did still. She had put herself in jeopardy.

He rowed quickly, came in close to the shore. She could see the boathouse and the cross. Soon the others would be down, for morning chapel. She wondered then what Cal would do about his wet clothes.

When he entered the dock underneath the cover of the boathouse, she handed him his watch. She could not see his face in the gloom, not with the sun off the water behind him, but she knew that he could see hers. She felt his fingers briefly in the exchange with the watch.

You're like me, he said to her.

When the others came for chapel, she was sitting on a bench already. A friend asked her why she had missed breakfast, and she answered that she'd gone for a walk. The others were noisy, took seats, changed seats. She leaned slightly sideways on her bench, her arm outstretched to prop her up, as if she were tired, waiting for the priest. In this way, she saved a space, so that when Cal came, she sat up straight and he sat down beside her. His hair was wet, but his shirt and pants were dry. They didn't speak.

The priest entered the clearing, stood beside the cross. The children rose and knelt and sat again. She looked out toward the water, noticed that the pink had turned to blue. Her hands were clasped loosely on her lap. She thought that she could feel the warmth of the boy through the sleeve of her blouse.

With one swift movement then, as if it had been rehearsed, thought about, practiced in the mind, the boy swept her hand off her lap and held it on the bench between them. His hand was cool and dry from the swimming, though she felt it tremble. He held her hand more tightly to stop the trembling. She felt something flutter deep inside her abdomen and knew that her face was hot. She looked at her feet, heard the priest intone his words. The water and the sun spun around her.

❦ ❦ ❦ ❦ ❦

THE SKY IS HEAVY AND GRAY, A FINE SNOW BEGINNING, like ashes from a fire. He has been waiting in the parking lot for more than half an hour, is worried that she won't arrive before the storm begins in earnest. He has listened to weather reports at least half a dozen times this morning, has determined that since the storm is moving in from the west, she's probably been in it for some time. The prediction is for heavy accumulation, the first substantial snow this season. His children at breakfast were hoping for a day off from school, though they will begin their Christmas vacation tomorrow. He thinks of Harriet in her pink flannel nightgown this morning, of the way she walked him to the door, wished him a good trip, worried over his driving in the bad weather, and he winces. He has had to tell her he had business in western Connecticut, will have to stay overnight.

He gets out of the car, buttons his overcoat, tucks in

his scarf. The parking lot is slippery; his shoes make elongated footprints in the thin wet covering. He walks to the neck of the drive, scans its length. It is the first night he and Siân will have together, the first time they will be able to sleep in the same bed. They've never even been together in the dark. Always before, she has had to leave shortly after lunch to get home to her daughter or to make supper. He feels like a man less than half his age who might never have been with a woman, the promise of an entire night sleeping next to a woman an incomparable gift. Yet even so, he senses as he always does the press of time, of minutes passing already, of a finite number of hours that he will be with Siân before she has to leave him; and that when she does leave him, time will stop, as if he were about to be executed. He remembers, as a boy, lying in his bed, trying to imagine what it would be like to be a condemned prisoner, watching the clock tick away the minutes left of life. It seemed to him the worst imaginable fate—to know precisely when one would die.

They have been together now four times, including their first lunch. Always, since that day, they have met here at the inn, gone straight to the room. He is known now, is greeted warmly on the phone when he calls for a reservation. The last two days they had together, the management put them into a suite that had at its entrance two successive locked doors; Siân joked immediately that they'd been put into a soundproof room. He aches with wanting her, and his body tightens. He looks at his watch for the tenth time in the half hour. He cannot think of her now without also seeing the erotic images they had created together: Siân with her back to him, pressed against a chaste, blue-flowered wallpaper; Siân in a hot bath, the room filled with steam (her glasses, until she took them off, opaque ovals), while he sat, fully dressed, on the lid of the toilet seat, drinking beer from a water glass, watching her breasts float above the waterline. Siân bending her neck while he unzipped her dress, the long line of her white back open to his hand. The muscle of her inner thigh made wet from both of them.

It is not so much, he knows, that he or she, or they together, are particularly skilled or adventurous; it is rather that their bodies want each other, fit, are trying to say something that cannot be said with words. He understands, too, that somehow, at least for the two of them, eros is linked with time. It is in the very urgency of time, the sense that their minutes together are short and numbered, that he must say what he has come to say before she leaves, that gestures and words cannot be wasted. But it is, paradoxically, also in the vast expanse of the lost years—the keen sense, whenever he is with her, of all the days and hours missed, the youthful bodies not known, the thousands of nights he might have touched her easily, without loss, without guilt and anxiety. They will never know together the sense of time squandered. To the contrary, he thinks of their hours together as time stolen or salvaged—time-outs from their separate realities.

He turns in his pacing, faces into the snow, walks in the direction of the parking lot. The inn, in the gloom of the lowered skies, is inviting, the door laced with holly, the windows lit with small electric candles on the sills. He has brought Siân a present, and he will give it to her this evening before they go down to dinner. This will be, will have to be, their Christmas together; he knows they will not be able to see each other again before Christmas, perhaps not again before the new year. He does not know how they will survive the holidays, and thinking this, he feels again the seaweed on the line, the drag of guilt, the chaos of facts and his inability to sort them out. He has a wife and three children—each blameless, each believing in the rituals of Christmas Eve and Christmas morning, each ignorant of his infidelity. He has betrayed his family in the absolute and common sense of desiring and sleeping with another woman, *loving* another woman, but he cannot escape the notion that he has betrayed them as well with the debacle of his financial ruin. Within days, unless he can work a deal at the bank, he will have to tell Harriet that they will not only lose the house and all their equity in it, but they will almost certainly have to declare bankruptcy to ward off the creditors who have been hounding him. He hardly knows which is worse—to tell her that he loves another woman or to tell her that he can no longer provide for her as he has promised to.

These large betrayals, he believes, will not be forgiven, but he sometimes wonders if it isn't the smaller betrayals that are worse. He thinks of the dozens of times in the past several weeks that he has lied to his wife: He left a Christmas party in their neighborhood twice last Saturday night, saying that he wanted to check up on the children, when what he actually did was drive to a phone booth to call Siân, who he knew was alone for the evening. ("This is torture," he remembers telling Siân that night.) He has surreptitiously poured milk down the sink, then told his wife that he would go to the store for her to make sure the kids had milk for breakfast (surely that cannot be forgiven, he thinks—the use of fatherly love in the service of adultery), when what he intended to do and did do was to drive to yet another phone booth and call his lover. He knows the location of every phone booth in his town and in the neighboring communities. He knows precisely at which phone booths he is likely not to be disturbed, which connect him immediately with AT&T, which are better to use during the day, which at night. He can punch in Siân's number and his credit card number in seconds, with or without his glasses, in the dark or in the light. He presses the numbers blind, like someone trying desperately to reach his drug dealer.

He wonders, too, not for the first time, how Siân manages in her own home. He can tell immediately, from the way she says hello on the telephone, whether or not her husband is present in the room when he calls. They have had dialogues that would be comical if they weren't so serious. He talks to her; he asks her questions; she responds obliquely as if answering a phone solicitation from a PBS television station or a political cause. He believes he has communicated more to her, said more to her, in the several weeks they have been together than he has ever shared with anyone.

Certainly he has never talked to his wife the way he talks to Siân.

He has never been inside Siân's home, but when he talks to her on the telephone, and when he thinks of her during the day (a continual series of images and thoughts, interrupted only by a momentary and strenuously willful effort to concentrate on a task at hand or a question posed to him), he tries to envision her life with her daughter and her husband. Sometimes he imagines her in a T-shirt and ponytail, leaning against the lip of a counter, holding a phone in one hand and preparing a meal with the other. Often, when he calls, he shares her attentions with Lily, her three-year-old, who seems to chatter constantly at her feet. He thinks she is a good mother; he likes the way she speaks to her daughter, speaks of her daughter. He has a less clear sense of what she is like as a wife. He cannot bring to focus the image of Siân sitting at a table with another man, embracing another man, lying in a bed with another man. He senses—she has allowed him to believe—that the marriage is not a good one, perhaps never was. She has alluded to an emptiness in the relationship, which he has seized upon and possibly embroidered; and he knows that he has extrapolated from her poetry a kind of deprivation, an emotional desert. She has said little of, and he has not asked about, her sexual life with her husband (though it is this question that haunts him, that seems always to be at the edge of his tongue when he is with her, that he is sometimes afraid that he will, despite his best intentions, ask), apart from her comment early on that she was "frozen."

Sometimes he hopes this means that she and her husband no longer make love; at other times he knows this can't possibly be true, and that knowledge sickens him. Is it really conceivable that she and her husband have not been together since he first kissed Siân?

He brushes the snow from the top of his head, stamps his feet to shake out the cold. He says aloud, once, the words "Screw it," as if by that he might ward off a sense of hopelessness that he feels coming upon him now, like gathering fog. He feels it particularly when his thoughts have led him to images of Siân with her child, in her home, or when he watches his own children in his own home. He does not want to imagine a life now without Siân, yet he cannot begin to sort out in his mind how a life with her will be accomplished. Even if he were able to walk away from Harriet and his children (which seems to him at times nearly as unimaginable as cutting off a foot), is it at all likely that Siân would do the same? Would she *want* to do the same? Would her husband just meekly leave the marriage and his farm? Impossible. Then what? Would Siân bring her daughter to Rhode Island to live with him? Could they live somewhere in between? And if so, what then of his business? Even as anemic as his business is, it is still grounded in a particular locale. If he's ever to salvage it, if he's ever to wait out the recession, it has to be done with the community. Or *would* it be possible to set up shop somewhere else?

He hears rather than sees the car coming—the slippery hiss of tires on the drive. He turns, she puts on the brakes; the car skids gently a foot or two. She rolls down the window, her face flushed with her impatience with the weather or (he hopes) with her impatience to be with him. He bends down, kisses her on the mouth. She smiles broadly; she seems as exhilarated as he is to have this whole day together.

"I thought you'd never get here," he says.

"I'd never not get here," she says.

He unlocks each of the double doors, follows her inside. There are electric candles at the windows, a fire in the fireplace, a large bowl of fruit on a table between the windows. She turns to him, a look of mild surprise on her face.

"Did they . . . ?"

He nods.

"They know," she says.

"Of course they know." He smiles. The fire and the fruit seem an omen—a sign that others have seen them together and approve. She takes off her coat, lets it slide into a heap on a chair. She has worn her hair pinned at the sides, and it falls loosely along her back. There is more gray at the temples than he has noticed before; she seems self-conscious about her hair, touches it, smooths back a strand. Her face is bright from the cold. She has worn a black dress with long sleeves. She sits on the chair, removes her leather boots. The melted snow from the soles and the heels make small puddles on the highly polished wood floor.

He kneels, buries his face in her lap. She puts her hands to the back of his neck, bends her head to his.

He feels the warmth of her thighs at either side of

his face, the soft wool of her dress on his cheeks. She is holding him as she might a child, and he wants to weep. What they want seems so simple—time together, a lifetime together, or what is left of a lifetime together—and yet that small goal, he knows, is fraught with endless complications: a maze of responsibilities and commitments, deceptions and betrayals. Why, why, why, he asks himself silently for the hundredth time, couldn't they have remained somehow connected—in touch, with all that the phrase implies—until they were old enough to find each other again? How maddening that they should have met when they were children and had no control over their lives.

His anger and his grief and his specific lust for this woman fill him with a need so sharp he shudders. He raises her skirt to her hips. He wants to devour her, and he is afraid that he might inadvertently hurt her. He lifts his face to hers so that she can see this. She touches his face with her hands. Perhaps he *is* weeping. He draws her down off the chair, onto the floor. He moves her skirt up toward her waist, slips off her underwear. He finds her with his tongue, kisses her, caresses her with his mouth. He waits for the tiny sound she makes at the back of her throat, a faint cry of helplessness, as from a small animal, and watches now the delicate arch of her white neck, her head thrust back, her mouth slightly open.

And when she comes, he thinks that possibly the most erotic image of all may be the tilt of her nostrils seen across the long expanse of her body.

* * *

"It's lovely," she says, turning once for him. The robe is short and silk, ivory, and barely covers her in the back, a fact that makes her laugh and blush at the same time. She sits on an upholstered chair, crosses her legs, and tries to look demure, a task she seems to know is hopeless. The robe falls open slightly, draped just so along the curve of her breasts, and she makes no move to close it. He likes sitting on the bed, looking at her in the robe. He enjoyed choosing it for her, thinking of her in it, though he knows she will have to conceal it when she goes home. He wishes they had a place of their own, however small, so that she could hang the robe in a closet and it would always be there. He wishes he could cook a wonderful meal for her.

"I love you," she says.

"I know."

"But I feel bad."

"Why?"

"I didn't bring you a present. There was nothing I could find that you could have taken home, that seemed to say what I want to say to you."

He ponders this. "What might you have gotten me that would have said what you wanted to say that I couldn't have taken home?"

She smiles, thinks. "A lake, maybe."

He laughs.

"Or a small country."

"Possibly this hotel?" he suggests.

"Perfect," she says. "Or a plane."

"A plane?"

"Mmmm. And flying lessons."

"I'd like a biplane. I've always wanted a biplane."

"Or years," she says.

"How many?"

"Thirty or so."

"Past or future?"

"Both. How many years do you think we have left?"

His heart leaps. She *does* think of them together. "My grandfather lived to be ninety-six," he says, "in full possession of all his faculties. *And* he drank Jack Daniel's and smoked half a pack a day."

"I've got it," she says, looking pleased with herself. "The ideal present. A videotape of us together here when we were kids. Of the whole week. What we sounded like. What we looked like."

He tries to imagine what she sounded like as a fourteen-year-old, wishes he could, for a moment, hear her voice. "We know what we looked like. From the picture. Anyway, I don't need a present. I don't want a present. Your being here is enough."

"It's not enough," she says.

"No. You're right. It's not."

She leans forward, folds her hands across her knee. "I wonder," she says, "if we had all the time in the world, if we knew we could be together for the rest of our lives, would we not care anymore, would we grow bored with each other—or fight?" She laughs.

"I doubt it," he says.

"We'll never know."

"Don't say that. Please."

"And I also wonder," she says, "if we *had* been together all this time, what would we be feeling now?

Would we be as happy as we are now? Would we even know what we had? Without having known the loss of it, I mean.,"

"I'd like to think we'd know," he says, "that we'd have known all along."

"You probably wouldn't have liked me when I was younger," she says. "You'd have thought me too stiff or too repressed or too serious or whatever. I was a virgin, technically, until I was twenty-two. And even then, I didn't really get it. I think my erotic life got lost or was buried somehow—possibly by the church. It's one of the reasons I won't send Lily, though Stephen's mother thinks I'm damning her."

"I lost my virginity when I was nineteen," he says. "It seemed late at the time."

He looks away, unwilling to linger on the image of Siân losing her virginity—at any age. "No," he says, turning back to her. "I'll tell you this: No matter when I'd met you in my lifetime, no matter when, I'd have left what I was doing or who I was with to be with you."

A flicker of alarm passes briefly across her brow.

Though he has thought of little else, and he knows now that she has to have thought of this too, they have never actually mentioned leaving their respective homes to be together.

"You know we have to be together," he says quietly.

She shakes her head. She says nothing.

"Siân."

She turns her face away. "Not now," she says. "Please."

He takes a breath, exhales. "All right," he says, "but you know we have to talk about this sometime."

"I just want this one night to be a happy one," she says. "Without complications. Or is that not possible?"

"I'm sorry," he says, getting off the bed and walking to the chair where she is sitting. "It will be."

He slides the robe gently off her shoulders so that it falls open and along her arms. He kneels, looks at her breasts. They are small and round. Below them there is the curve of her abdomen—from her babies. He bends forward, kisses her belly, then her left breast.

"Is this the one?" he asks.

"What one?"

"On the bench, that first day."

She thinks a minute. "Yes, I suppose it is." She gathers the robe across her chest, covering herself.

"They're small," she says.

He looks at the crumple of fabric where she is holding it with her hand. "Well, look at it this way," he says. "They'll never sag."

She laughs. "Yes they will."

"No they won't."

He bends to her again.

"They're little," he says, "but I know for a fact they like to be kissed."

"Mr. Callahan."

The maître d' nods at Charles, indicates that he should follow him to what has become, in the several weeks they have been visiting the inn, their table. The snow outside the windows is thinning out; the storm, it seems, is nearly over. Charles follows Siân across the long dining room, his hand lightly at her waist. She has worn her hair down; it falls in a loose fan along the back of her dress. Pearls circle her neck. Charles orders immediately, as he has planned, a bottle of champagne.

They sit side by side, and he takes her hand. Siân crosses her legs, touches a heavy silver spoon. He surveys the room. Only three other tables are occupied tonight; he suspects that the storm has kept most people away, though he has never eaten here in the evening. Instead of flowers in the center of the room, there is a Christmas tree—a small, simple tree with white lights. Boughs of spruce, interspersed with white candles, decorate the fireplace mantel.

"Pretty," he says.

She nods. Her mood seems altered, shaded.

"What's wrong?" he asks.

She shakes her head. "Nothing's wrong."

"You seem pensive."

She smiles. "It *is* pretty. I'm sorry."

The waiter brings the champagne, pops the cork, fills the glasses. Charles raises his to Siân.

"To presents we can't give each other," he says.

"Yet," she says.

She takes a sip, doesn't meet his eyes. She puts her glass down.

"What's it like?" she asks. "Your Christmas?"

He sighs. So that's why she is pensive. He studies her mouth, the long curve of her lower lip. "Are you sure you want to hear this?" he asks. "It might be better if we didn't."

"No, I'm sure. I'd like to be able to picture what you're doing that evening, that day."

He hesitates. He has a feeling that he has often: a sense that no matter how he answers this question, the answer will be the wrong one. "Are you writing?" he asks instead.

She turns her head slightly away. She seems surprised by the question. "Not much," she says. "I write to you. I can't work well now. I'm too . . . preoccupied, I guess you would say."

"I know the feeling."

"You're trying to change the subject."

"OK. OK. Here's what happens. My wife's parents and my parents and my wife's sister and her kids come over on Christmas Eve, and basically I hang out in the kitchen, cooking."

"You have Christmas on Christmas Eve."

"The adults do. We open our presents in the evening, after the children are in bed. The kids open theirs in the morning."

"Oh. And do you go to church?"

"I don't. And Harriet doesn't . . ." A flicker of something crosses Siân's eyes. He wishes he hadn't mentioned his wife by name. ". . . but my parents go to midnight mass, and maybe my daughter Hadley will go with them. I'm usually doing the dishes."

She is silent next to him. He knows what she is picturing, what she is imagining, what she wants to ask and won't: Do he and his wife exchange presents? When do they do this: when others are present or when they are alone? He watches as she drains her glass, pushes it forward on the table as though to ask for another. Silently he fills her glass again. She raises it, nearly drains it at one go.

"Siân . . . ," he says.

"Do you want to hear about my Christmas rituals? So you can picture what I'm doing."

"Siân, don't," he says.

"It's quite interesting. Really, Charles, you should let me tell you."

There is a slightly manic note to her voice that he has never heard before. She drains her glass, nudges it forward yet again. "The champagne is delicious," she says. "You have excellent taste. I feel like getting drunk tonight. Why not."

Reluctantly he fills her glass again. "Why don't we order?" he suggests.

"In a minute," she says. "I'm going to tell you about Christmas Eve on a Polish onion farm. You haven't lived until you've had Christmas on a Polish onion farm."

"Siân, why are you doing this?"

"Actually, I used to like this ritual. I used to like rituals of any kind to break the silences. I used to like as many people in the house as possible. . . ."

"Let's talk about something else."

"It's called Wigilia," she says, "the Christmas Eve dinner. We have it at our place, all the relatives—well, all Stephen's side of the family. We visit my father the day after Christmas. I cook for days beforehand with Stephen's mother. I bet you can't picture that, can you, his mother and me in the kitchen, making pirogis.

Well, I do. You can't imagine how good they are. You like to cook. You should learn how to make them. . . ."

"Siân."

"I fill them with sauerkraut or potato or farmer's cheese and potato or prunes. The prune ones are especially delicious. . . ."

"We can go upstairs, come down later to eat if you want," he says. Her face is flushed, her eyes too bright.

"And we never have meat. Only fish. We have pickled herring. Do you like pickled herring? And pike and carp. And borscht. And sometimes cabbage soup. And sauerkraut and sardines. And a kind of poppyseed bread. And figs and dates. And everybody eats as much as he can. And oh, I almost forgot: You have to leave a place for the unknown visitor. You know who the unknown visitor is, don't you?"

He looks about across the long dining room. The heavy white linen seems extraordinarily beautiful to him—comforting, weighed down by anchors of silver. When he turns to glance outside the long windows, he sees that the snow has finally stopped. Within the dining room, and without, there is an unearthly quiet, the quiet of a building surrounded by a new snow. And is it only his imagination, or is everyone in the room actually frozen, listening intently to Siân's voice, at once animated and brittle, as if it were a piece of crystal that might soon shatter?

"Well, it's for Jesus Christ. That's who."

She puts her glass down on the table. She stands up slowly, with inordinate care, and slips through the small space between the banquette tables, as though each movement had been choreographed. She turns delicately without looking at him. He watches her walk the long distance through the dining room, her pace unhurried, her back straight. Her heels click rhythmically on the wooden floor. He follows her with his eyes until she rounds a corner and he can see her no more.

The champagne was a mistake. They have not eaten all day. He will give her a minute, then follow her back to the room. Perhaps she ought to have a short nap before they eat. He will suggest it, rub her back. The dining room must be open late; he'll speak to the maître d'. He knew it was risky territory; he tried to warn her off. And yet, he thinks, this had to happen. It's his own anger too. At what might have been and wasn't. Will he ever be able to listen to her talk about her life, or she his, without the hurt?

He looks up. A waiter is at his elbow.

"I'm sorry, sir," the man says, "but I thought you'd like to know."

"Know what?"

"Your friend appears to be ill."

Charles stands up. "Where is she?"

"She's in the ladies' room, sir."

He finds her kneeling in a stall, her feet splayed out behind her. A waitress, standing in the center of the room as if not wanting to approach any nearer, is the only other person present. Charles nods to the waitress, dismisses her. "I'll handle this," he says.

Siân retches once into the basin, reaches up with her hand to flush the toilet. Charles moves in beside her, squats down with his back against the stall. Siân's face is white, with pearls of sweat on her forehead. He holds her hair back with one hand, puts the other to her forehead to brace her.

"It's all right," he tells her. "Let it out. Let it go. Don't fight it." It is what he tells his children when they are sick in the night.

"I can't do this," she cries. "I can't do this."

"It's OK, Siân. It's OK."

"No, it's not OK. It's not OK at all. My daughter is at home without me. I have to lie all the time. We didn't have all those years, and now it's too late, we won't be able to have any time at all. We have families, and they need us."

"We'll work it out," he says quietly.

She retches again into the bowl, wipes her mouth. He flushes the toilet for her.

She sits back against a corner of the stall, her knees raised. She doesn't seem to care about her ungainly posture, her knees spread as if she had on jeans and were resting against a stone wall. He takes a handkerchief from his suit pocket, hands it to her. Her face is bathed in sweat, her hair curling along its edges in wet tendrils. In the fluorescent light, her face washed of color, she looks every bit of her forty-six years—a middle-aged woman, he would say now—and curiously, studying her, he can see all of her, all the women she has been or will be, from the young girl to the old woman. The clarity of the images frightens him, but he is aware only that he loves her, that he wants nothing more in life than to be allowed to take care of her.

"You don't understand," she says, her eyes rimmed

red, her cheeks wet. She reaches up for toilet paper, blows her nose. "My husband gets up early and makes doughnuts on Christmas morning. He's giving me a leather-bound edition of my book. On Christmas morning, we drape a blanket across the entrance to the living room, so that Lily can't peek at her presents, and then we ceremoniously drop the blanket, and she squeals with delight. My daughter loves Polish food. Even I like the pirogis. Don't you see? We can't undo that."

Her voice has reached a pitch he has never heard before. He watches as she leans her head back, sighs deeply.

"I'm finished," she says. She closes her eyes. She looks worn, exhausted. "Families once took us away from each other, and now families are taking us away from each other again."

"I'll help you," he says.

She shakes her head. "You can't help me," she says quietly. "Neither one of us can help the other, and that's the truth."

He lifts her to her feet. He watches while she washes her face at the sink, towels it dry. She sloshes mouthfuls of water, spits them out. She runs her fingers through her hair, pulling the wet strands back.

"I need some fresh air," she says.

"I know," he says. "I'll get our coats."

He returns from the room with their coats and scarves and her boots. She exchanges her shoes for her boots in the hallway.

"Wait here," he says to her before they go outside. "I'll be right back."

When he rejoins her in the hallway, he is carrying a broom.

"I got it from the kitchen," he says.

"What's it for?"

"You'll see."

Outside, the snow across the lawn is a vast cascade of white, unmarred by footsteps of any kind. He calculates, as they make their way down to the path, that the accumulation must be somewhere between four and six inches. A moon has risen and shines through the last patches of cloud. It will be a clear night and cold.

He takes her arm, helping her through the snow. Her boots are dress boots with heels, not meant for hiking. When they are halfway down the lawn, he turns to see the inn behind them. The facade is ablaze, the glow from inside making golden pools of light on the snow. In the darkness, it seems as if inside the inn there were a large party, a Christmas party, with many guests dressed in velvet and gold and black, holding champagne glasses, smiling under holly, their faces lit by candlelight. He has a fleeting sense of having left something important and warm behind.

Amidst the pines, the going is rougher, the light from the moon partially obscured. Beside him, Siân has begun to breathe more normally. He carries the broom over his shoulder like a rifle.

When they reach the clearing, they can just make out the shape of the benches in the snow. He walks with Siân to the one closest to the lake, the one they sat on a few weeks ago, brushes it off with the broom.

"That's what the broom was for?" she asks.

"No, not exactly," he replies.

She sits on the bench, her hands in the pockets of her coat, her body drawn inward against the cold.

"I'm going to test the ice," he says.

The snow on the lake is faintly blue from the moon. He is not sure exactly where the shoreline ends and the lake begins, but when he reaches the ice, the soles of his shoes slip against the hard surface. He is destroying his shoes, he knows, and his feet are frozen from the snow. He walks twenty-five feet out onto the surface of the lake, takes a test jump; the ice feels solid. He begins then to sweep. The snow, so new and light, blows effortlessly away like dust. When he has cleared a patch the size of a small bedroom, he slips across his newly created rink and walks to where Siân is sitting.

"We're going to walk on water," he says, reaching for her hand.

"You're crazy," she says.

"Well, we knew that."

He holds her hand, then her whole arm when they reach the ice. She makes one small tentative movement onto the ice, leans into him for support. When he takes her weight, he is afraid for a moment that his footing will give and they might both go down, but his shoes hold and he steadies her. Together they slide forward, first one foot and then the other.

He lets go of her arm, but not her hand. They glide across the ice, she occasionally clutching him when she feels herself about to lose her balance. They are dark shapes on the lake; he can barely see her face.

"I'll always love you," she says.

"I know," he says.

A bird—an owl?—hoots at them from across the lake. But the snow, all round them, is a buffer, smothering the sounds of the outside world.

In the center of the small square he has made, he turns to her, then holds her arm out in the classic dance posture. They execute a few slippery steps, draw closer to each other for support.

"What are you listening for?" she asks.

"You won't believe this," he says.

"I might."

"The Brahms Second Piano Concerto. Do you know it?"

"I think so. Where are you?"

"I'm in the third movement. The quiet one. The one that begins with the cello."

"Oh."

"It's a concerto, but it's like a symphony," he says. "I used to think it was the most beautiful piece of music I'd ever heard, and I'm not sure I don't still think that. Sometimes, when everyone is out of the house, I put it on full blast and just luxuriate in it. I believe it's the longest concerto ever written. Brahms himself was the soloist at its premiere. God, how I'd love to have heard that. I have a number of versions, but I'm partial to Cliburn with the Chicago Symphony Orchestra. Although the Rudolf Serkin is absolutely—"

"Charles."

She puts her gloved hands to his face.

"What?"

"Stop."

"Stop?"

"You're as bad as I am with the Polish food."

Her face is white, drained by the moon. She looks, despite her warm coat and scarf and gloves, naked to him, her face unmasked, her eyes, in the cool light, black and open. This is, he knows, one moment that they have, one moment in time, one pearl on a short string.

"If you're skating on thin ice," he whispers into the frosty night, "you might as well dance."

Around the curtains there is light. They are naked in the bed, she folded into him, like spoons. He is hard when he awakens, knows it instantly, knows too that this is not generic lust, that she was there in the dissipating dream: He sees her face in a fragment before it drifts away. He finds her breast, the small nipple, nearly always erect. Her belly, the softness there. She does not exercise, and, somehow, this appeals to him. He makes a light circular motion with his hand, and she awakens, turns onto her back. He knows he must look like a pterodactyl, his thinning hair in a sculpture all its own, but she smiles, embraces him, shifts slightly so that in one movement he is above her. He enters her immediately without needing to be guided in. She is slippery already, as though waiting for him in her dream. *Was* it a dream that produced this, he wonders, or is it left from an earlier time—how many hours ago?—in the night? He straddles her legs; he feels welded to her, and he can see her face. Her excitement is contagious, fuels his own, as his, he knows, triggers hers. He watches now as her mouth opens; he circles her tongue with his own. He smooths her hair from her forehead. He raises himself up, his weight on his hands. Her eyes dart from his face to his shoulder and back again. He watches as a flush of color begins at her throat, suffuses her face. They are locked in a deep, slow rhythm, the ebb and flow of waves. In time, studying her, he sees the slight arch of her neck that tells him she is close. He has wondered if it might be possible, but now it seems almost inevitable. He feels himself there, holds back, examines the tilt of her chin. In a few hours they will leave each other, sucked back into lives of lost meaning. There is only this now; this is everything. The frame of the world around them increases his urgency. He waits for her to close her eyes, as she almost always does near the end, but this time, she opens them immediately, astonishing him.

"I want to see you," she whispers.

And saying that, she comes, and he is with her, and it is only seconds later that he hears again the mingled bewilderment and pleasure of their simultaneous cries.

$\mathcal{J}$t was brief, and yet it was a lifetime. I used to think it was something I would never have, that the era in which I was raised and the church I nearly wed had bred it out of me, or had leached it out. But you gave it to me, or I gave it to you, and now I cannot separate your body from your words, nor mine from my thoughts. I cannot separate what we did from who we were. Every image is erotic, or within the fold, etched in stone now, engraved blossoms.

In December, the black dirt held the warmth long after the other soil had frozen, as if, along with the light, the dirt had swallowed up the sun. Consequently, the early snows melted on the onion fields, like snow falling into the sea.

That December, I touched my daughter often. Stephen worked on machinery and taught at the school, and when we chanced upon each other, in the kitchen or in a hallway, he held himself away from me, in self-preservation. I believe now that he knew before I did that I was leaving him, that he felt it in the silences, in the unbreachable distance, even as he denied it to himself, refused to imagine it.

We spoke sometimes and were careful with each other—unwilling yet to disturb the separate peace each of us had made.

The week before Christmas, I went into the attic, where I had found your picture, and brought out garlands and tinsel, colored lights and a star. The ornaments were heavy, the garlands weighted, and it was an effort to raise my arms to the tree. Lily asked me often what it was I was looking at, and I answered her that I wasn't looking, I was thinking.

I was thinking about equations: Is one hour spent doing X equal to thirty-one years of doing Y?

On Christmas morning, my husband left the bed early. I waited until I could smell the fried dough and the coffee, and I went down to join him. He was wearing an ocher flannel shirt, and I was thinking: Are you wearing a similar shirt, one that I have never seen, may never see at all? Are you with your wife, your children? Do you hold your wife in the bed when you sleep? Do your children join you in the bed on Christmas morning, making a sandwich of bodies, as Stephen and I sometimes did with Lily and had done with Brian when Brian was with us?

It wasn't possible, of course, ever to forget Brian, or that he should have been there with us. Christmas was the worst, though I don't know how I can say that. Every day was the worst; the pain was not dulled by time, not filled up, not muted. He had died in a friend's car on the way home from a soccer game at school, died when the car in which he was traveling was hit by a metallic-blue Corvette that had run the light. In the few seconds just before the intersection, the last few seconds of his life, Brian, for reasons that will never be known to us, had unfastened his seat belt. For days, for weeks, for months afterward, I replayed that scene in my head, willing time to stop, so that I could crawl into that car, into the back seat, and refasten the seat belt for my son.

Stephen finished frying the doughnuts. In his flannel shirt, he made an effort to be festive. Lily came, with a bright anticipatory smile. With a flourish, Stephen let down the curtain, and Lily ran to the tree.

We ate the doughnuts as Lily opened up her stocking and her presents. Stephen and I made a show for each other, each pretending to be happy. I opened the leather book: It was beautiful, and I said so. I had given Stephen an easel and a set of costly oil paints, and I saw at once the confusion behind his smile: How could he take up again this hobby while he was under siege?

We were sitting in the living room, awash with colored paper, toys underfoot. Stephen made a fire, brought us more coffee. I was thinking that in each house on the street, in all the pastel houses, there were children and colored paper, and women and men who might or might not love each other, who might or might not have indelible connections of their own. And it was then that I remembered another present for Lily, one I had hidden away. It was a sweater, a rose-colored sweater that she could wear through the winter.

I laughed. I've forgotten a present, I said.

Stephen said, You do this every year.

I said, I hide them so well I sometimes forget about them. I'll just get it now.

Stephen was standing. No, I'll get it, he said. I'm already up.

I looked at him against the window, the overbright light from the snow outside causing him to be in silhouette.

Yes, OK, I said. It's in the dresser in my closet, the third drawer down.

I sat back, took a sip of coffee. Lily had on her lap a jewelry box with a secret compartment that intrigued her. The hot coals from the fireplace filled the room with warmth.

I sat up quickly then; the coffee spilled onto my robe. I was paralyzed, unable to speak or move. Lily said, Mum, you spilled your coffee.

I waited a minute, possibly an hour. I heard Stephen's footsteps through the kitchen, looked over to where he stood in the doorway.

I saw it all on his face—that peculiar mix of confusion and horror that accompanies a fear confirmed.

In his hands he held your shirt.

❦ ❦ ❦ ❦ ❦ ❦

THE WIND FROM THE NORTHEAST RIPS ALONG HIGH
Street, stinging the side of his face with a cold rain that
smells of the sea. Charles watches as a string of Christmas lights loops high over the traffic, dislodging a
wreath, which bounces once onto the street, then
scuds along the sidewalk like prairie sage. Last-minute
shoppers, their faces pinched with cold, bend toward
the storm. From his vantage point on the top step of
the bank, Charles looks out over the row of storefronts
toward the harbor. Even sheltered, the water is rough;
a grizzled sky meets a muddy sea not two hundred feet
from shore, obliterating the lighthouse at the end of the
point. He hopes each of the draggermen has made it
back in; there is nothing worse than a boat late or lost
over Christmas. He remembers two or three scares
from the past, the news spreading with Christmas
greetings until no one in town could pass a window
without looking out to sea and mumbling a prayer—as

though no celebration could begin until all boats were in and accounted for.

The storm will hurt the shops, he thinks, the small businesses struggling through the worst Christmas season in memory. Already McNamara, with his lumberyard at the end of High Street, has declared bankruptcy; and Janet Costa, at the stationery store, has told Harriet she won't make it through February. The decline is contagious, the failure of each enterprise a harbinger of other failures to come. Charles wonders if the street soon will resemble a ghost town, with rows of empty storefronts.

He takes one step down, hikes his collar to cover his ears. He should go home, he knows, to help Harriet with the tree, but if he goes now, he is certain she will see it on his face—their own failure, *his* failure. He feels the anger, but oddly there is now as well a kind of relief. It can't get much worse, and in that there is some comfort. The particular struggle to save his house is over.

He looks across at the coffee shop; he could go in there, get himself a sandwich, wish a few clients a happy Christmas. But it isn't what he wants—it won't take the edge off the anger. He looks down the street in the direction of The Blue Schooner: a pint, a bowl of hot chowder, wish a different set of clients a happy Christmas. The wind howls up the steps, buffets his coat. Nothing keeps out the cold in a storm like this, he knows. He feels the raw air inside his sleeves and close to his chest.

Hunched in his coat, he jogs down the steps of the

bank. On the sidewalk, he turns to look up at the imposing edifice. The thick white columns support a wide stone portico. An oversize wreath, decorated with tiny jewels of light and golden bows, hangs over tall wooden doors, as if promising access inside to wealth and taste and power, when what the bank has really done is suck the town dry. Charles wants to give the bank the finger, suppresses this juvenile urge.

He hates the bank, The Bank, the institution itself and not really the people who work inside it. He hates the institution that has siphoned millions of dollars out of the community with its stock offerings that have all gone to shit, the one that has lent out other millions and now lost all of it. He can't even count the number of people in town who've had to forfeit, in the last several months, their retirements, their IRAs, everything they had. Now the bank has no money to lend to keep people like Medeiros afloat—literally.

The meeting was brief, stunningly brief and clearly pointless. Whalen had called the meeting deliberately for the twenty-fourth, and Charles knew this was punishment for his having crossed the banker at the volleyball game. He felt sorry now for that encounter; he knew the financial fiasco wasn't Whalen's fault, and when Charles arrived at the bank—twenty minutes late for his eleven o'clock appointment (twenty deliberate minutes spent sitting in the Cadillac in the bank's parking lot; they could all be children when they wanted to be)—he wanted to say that to the banker. Charles studied the sweating pink face, the remarkable shine on the bald pate, and said simply, "Whalen."

Whalen looked down at the papers on his desk, shuffled them. "You're four months behind on your mortgage payments, Callahan," he said. "What are you going to do about it?"

Charles knew immediately he shouldn't have come. What was the point of talking to Whalen anyway? If the bank was going to foreclose, then let it be. The process was inevitable. "You know I can't bring it up to date," he said.

Whalen looked at Charles. The man's reading glasses enlarged his pupils. Charles thought idly of hot frogs on a railroad track, felt truly sorry for the man. "The bank examiners are looking over our shoulders right now," Whalen said, "and they're forcing us to act on all our problem loans."

Charles felt his own face grow warm. He knew he should shrug his shoulders, walk out the door. It was what any sensible man would do. Or perhaps he should beg, plead the Christmas season; or lie, say the money would be there the first of the year. But why lie? There wouldn't be any money in January, or in February, for that matter.

"I know it's not your fault," Charles said. "I know you're only doing your job. To tell you the truth, Ed, I feel sorrier for you than I do for myself."

Whalen looked sick, even in the glow of incandescent light and warm wood. Charles knew that when the feds got through with Whalen, he, too, would be out on the street, and possibly on his way to jail.

Charles leaves the bank, passes the coffee shop, then makes his way toward The Blue Schooner. A Salvation Army Santa is out in front of the Woolworth's. Charles gives the can some change. A pickup truck passes, a wreath on its grille. Charles ponders what degree of holiday spirit would possess a man to put a Christmas wreath on his car, decides it must have something to do with kids. Halfway to The Blue Schooner, he comes upon a pair of phone booths on the sidewalk. He cannot pass a phone booth now without studying it, considering the possibilities. Generally he does not ever call her from a place as public as the center of town, but today everyone is so huddled, warding off the storm, that he is certain no one would notice him. Yet even so, he thinks again, it is too risky. They have agreed, tentatively, not to call each other all day Christmas Eve or on Christmas itself, with the understanding that neither is likely to be alone. He stops at the booth, looks at the black phone. He wants to tell her about Whalen, about losing his house. He wants to tell her that he thinks about her every minute, even when he is dealing with the bank; she is always there, hovering in his thoughts. He tries to imagine her in her kitchen, making pirogis with her mother-in-law. He picks up the receiver, puts it back. He leans on the shelf. How bad could it be? Even if the mother-in-law is there, or Lily is there, she could talk to him for just a minute, just long enough so that he could hear her voice, so that he could tell her that he thinks her feet are beautiful. He wants to hear her laugh. He picks up the phone again, dials the familiar number. The phone rings twice, three times, four times. He wonders idly where she is. At the store? Out in the car with her daughter? Is it raining there too, or snowing?

The phone stops ringing. He hears a man say hello. The man sounds breathless, as if he had run in from outside. The man says hello again, and Charles is paralyzed, unable to speak, unable to put the phone down. Once again the man at the other end says hello, this time with exasperation. The voice is deep; the "hello" has resonance. And yet the man does not sound cheerful or friendly, or is Charles extrapolating again, reading too much into a simple greeting? Charles hangs up the phone and backs away from the booth as if he had been barked at, nipped at, by a dog. He has imagined her husband, has known on one level that the man must exist, and yet the image has been disembodied, willed away when he wants it to be gone. But this he cannot will away—the resonance of that voice across the wire. The man does exist, is standing in her kitchen. Where *is* she?

Subdued and frustrated, he enters The Blue Schooner. The bar is thick with men, off early from work, in now from the water, or simply escaping the ennui of a day at home with no structure. Charles makes his way through the wet heat of the crush, finds Medeiros on a stool at the end of the bar. Charles hesitates, says hello.

"Callahan."

"Joe."

"Buy you a beer?"

"Thanks."

Medeiros is sweating under his wool cap. His eyes

are rheumy in the dim light. Medeiros will be going home to a Portuguese meal with his clan—squid and octopus; each family has its rituals. Charles leans on the bar, unbuttons his coat, shakes it out. He loosens his tie. The beer is sharp and cold, deeply satisfying. He returns the favor, orders Medeiros a bourbon.

"What's the matter, Callahan? You look like shit. You been losin' weight, or what?"

"Something like that."

"The kids OK?"

"The kids are fine."

"The wife?"

Charles starts to smile. "The wife is fine," he says.

"So what's the story, then? You broke?"

"Yeah, I'm broke."

Medeiros takes a long swallow of bourbon, looks at Charles. "Yeah, so what else is new? We're all broke. There's something else. You in trouble?"

Charles looks up at the ceiling, down at the condensation on his glass. He drains his beer, signals the bartender for another.

"You could say that, Joe. You could say I'm in trouble."

"I knew it. I knew you were in trouble. I told Antone you was in trouble. I could see it on your face. With the government? With the IRS? With that deal that went sour? What?"

Charles leans on his elbow, looks at Medeiros. "I'm in love."

Joe Medeiros seems stunned, stupefied by Charles's words—as if he hadn't heard a man say those words in a very long time, cannot quite compute them. The draggerman looks embarrassed, takes a thoughtful sip of bourbon. He shakes his head, out of his depth.

"I didn't figure you for that, Charlie. I never figured you for chasin' skirts."

"This isn't chasing skirts."

"Who is she?"

"No one you know."

"Where is she?"

"With her husband and daughter in Pennsylvania."

"Wow. Shit."

"Yeah. Shit."

"Does the wife know?"

"Harriet? No."

"You gonna tell her?"

"I don't know, Joe. I'm not sure what I'm going to do."

Medeiros looks away over the noisy crowd, as if pondering Charles's options. Defeated by the lack of easy solutions, he turns back to Charles.

"Well," Medeiros says, settling on a bromide, "you gotta do what your heart tells you."

Medeiros lets out a long sigh, acknowledging that even that was complicated. What if the heart wanted the lover but wanted the wife and kids not to be hurt?

"I guess," he adds lamely.

"Yeah, I guess," says Charles.

Medeiros looks at Charles, slides off his stool, not wanting to be in the proximity of such a thorny problem—not on Christmas anyway. "I gotta talk to Tony over there, find out his boats made it in,"

Medeiros says. He puts a hand on Charles's shoulder. "Hang in there," he says.

"Thanks, Joe. Have a happy Christmas."

Charles takes Joe's stool, orders a bowl of chowder. The chowder tastes good; nothing better than Rhode Island chowder, with its thin broth. He orders another pint of beer, listens to the cacophony in the room. The bar is close, overheated, redolent of damp wool from the fishermen's caps and jackets. A dozen clients are at tables or standing at the bar. Last Christmas—and at Christmases before that—Charles used the occasion to spread goodwill, rekindle contact with lapsing clients. But today he knows he cannot manage that. He feels disoriented, shut off from the men, shut out from a world in which the usual standards and words apply. The voices in the room seem overly loud, out of sync with the mouths forming the words, as if a sound track were a split second off. Charles shakes his head to clear it. He doesn't belong in here. He has to get out, but he can't go home either. Not yet.

Charles crosses the street, walks back toward the car. He is wet inside from sweating in the overheated bar; soaked outside from the nasty weather. He bends into the wind, watches as a car's spray washes along the street. Already the traffic is thinning out, everyone off work early, closing shops, going home. He was supposed to pick up something for Harriet—what? He tries to concentrate. Milk? Eggs? Bacon? Paper towels?

He reaches the bank parking lot, puts his key in the lock. As he does so, he glances over the top of the Cadillac, sees the back of St. Mary's, the town's Catholic church. He removes the key from the lock, crosses the lot, then makes his way through a wet mossy cemetery. He enters the church by a side door.

He hasn't been inside the church in over a year, not since the Fahey funeral. The interior is dimly lit, with electric lanterns high overhead. Votive candles flicker in bubbly red glasses. He walks in twenty feet, looks at the altar, nearly smothered today in poinsettias. He has always hated poinsettias; their color alone seems poisonous to him. He studies the cross suspended above the altar, a particularly grotesque crucifixion, the skin of Christ abnormally white, with magenta blood from the wounds dripping along the feet and hands. Why do this to children? he wonders, not for the first time. He walks to the front pew, sits down, his hands folded limply in his lap. He examines the cross on the altar itself, a simpler gold cross, without a body. He focuses on the cross, tries to formulate a prayer. But the old words still do not work, and he cannot create the necessary sentences. He wants to ask for help and to kneel, as if in those simple acts he might be forgiven— not so much for what he has done as for what he is about to do. His longing for forgiveness feels enormous, a large indefinable longing, but he knows the request is futile. He will never give up Siân; therefore, according to the rules of the game, asking for forgiveness is out of the question. And in any event, it has been too long since he has had any clear idea of what or whom he was asking for forgiveness.

A chill shakes him. He stands up to leave, glances again at the flickering votive candles, remembers now what it was he was supposed to get for Harriet: light bulbs. He hurries to the car. He has been gone too long. He needs to get home, be with his children. And Christ, he forgot: the ducks—he has to marinate the ducks.

Pulling into his driveway, he sees the twinkling Christmas tree behind the window of the family room. At least Harriet has finished the lights, he thinks, emerging guiltily from the car. When he enters the kitchen, his children and his dog run in to greet him. His children's love is physical; they climb up his legs, tug on his arms—even Hadley, who snuggles into his shoulder. They squeal at him that he is wet and that his coat smells from the damp. As he removes his coat and jacket, he gently shakes off his children, one by one. He slips his tie through his collar, rolls his sleeves, and squats to nuzzle Winston's head in affection.

The children lead him into the family room to admire the tree. Harriet is perched on a stool, trying to repair the star atop the tree; it lists to port. She has on jeans, a hunter-green sweater. He studies her broad shoulders, the swell of her hips below her sweater, the way the jeans pinch in at the crotch. But when he looks at her, he feels nothing, not even a certainty of what her body looks like beneath her clothes. Sometimes he cannot even remember what it was like to make love to Harriet, what it was they did together, as if his time with Siân had somehow erased that particular loop. He watches his wife's sweater ride up in back as she reaches again for the top of the tree. He studies the sliver of pink skin above her waistband. The skin seems foreign to him, skin he has never touched.

"Let me get that," he says behind her.

"Oh," she says, turning to him, flushed with her effort. "Thanks."

"I got the light bulbs," he says.

She steps off the stool. They exchange places.

"How did your appointment go?" she asks.

"Fine," he says. "It went fine."

He hasn't told her yet about the bank. At breakfast he announced only that he had an appointment. The ubiquitous and generic "appointment."

"You've been gone awhile," she says, looking at her watch. "I was worried you wouldn't get home in time to do the ducks."

"Had to buy a couple of rounds. You know how it is at Christmas."

Charles secures the star with picture wire. It's still off five degrees, but it will do.

"How have the kids been?" he asks, stepping off the stool, facing her.

She stares at him a moment, puts a finger to his chest, strokes the cloth of his shirt in the vicinity of his left nipple. Idly, as though lost in a memory. Her eyes are uncharacteristically vacant, staring at the skin above the top button of his shirt.

"Harriet."

She looks up at him, dragged reluctantly from her reverie. Her eyes are a vivid blue-violet and large—her best features. He has sometimes thought her pretty; she *is* pretty. But not beautiful. He tries to remember if he ever told her she was beautiful. Perhaps at the beginning. He must have then. He hopes he did.

"Jack is in orbit," she says slowly, removing her finger from his chest. "Hadley has been helping me with the tree. She wants to make cookies when you've finished with the ducks and the pâté."

She opens her mouth again, then closes it. She seems to want to say something more, something that is hard for her to say, and he knows that if she does, he will have to tell her. He wants to tell her that he is sorry, that whatever has happened or not happened between them, it was not her fault. That it wasn't because she wasn't beautiful or that he didn't want to love her. Or that he has been recognized, at last, in a way his wife has never known him. He puts his hand on the sleeve of her sweater, rubs her arm between her elbow and her shoulder.

She moves away from him, turns her face to the side. "Keep your eye on Anna," she says. "I have one or two more presents to wrap."

"Harriet?"

"Yes?"

She looks at him, wary now, the vacant look gone entirely. She narrows her eyes, seems almost irritated, impatient to leave the room.

"My parents will be here at four," she says.

Handel's *Messiah* blasts from the kitchen speakers. He has played it so often through the years that he knows almost all the words by heart. He likes particularly to belt out the "Hallelujah" chorus and does so as he puts the ingredients for the marinade—teriyaki sauce, fresh ginger, soy sauce, garlic, shallots, sherry, and a splash of red wine—into the several roasting bags. He has cut the breasts and legs and thighs off six ducks; purple carcasses line the yellow Formica kitchen counter. Winston stands by his feet, his nose pointed upward, alert for a tidbit that might deliberately fall his way. Somewhere between the second and third ducks, Charles sliced the tip of a finger; he has stanched the bleeding with a kitchen towel, which is now wrapped untidily around his hand. Hadley, leaning against the counter, studies her father thoughtfully. He glances down at her face, at the steady gaze of her large brown eyes. She looks concerned.

"Dad," she says.

"What?"

"Are you all right?"

He slides duck pieces into a roasting bag with a flourish, sets it along with the other bags in a large pan on the counter. He is on a roll now, four cookbooks open on the island. His menu did not really come together until somewhere between "O thou that tellest . . ." and "All we like sheep . . . ," and he has been into town twice for extra ingredients for his meal—once to the fish market, once to the Italian deli—emptying his checking account in the process. He is aware that his menu is somewhat eclectic and that possibly all of the proper components are not quite there, but he has always preferred to cook because he felt like making the separate dishes, not necessarily because they formed a perfect whole—and he thinks that somehow this spontaneous and haphazard desire might be applicable to his life and his financial ruin as well. In addition to the duck carcasses on the counter, he has now two fillets of salt cod for the baccalà; five pounds of mussels (he hadn't planned on the mussels, but he couldn't pass them up at the fish store—he will serve them in a brine of tomato, basil, capers, and white wine); one fillet of salmon, which he will coat with salt and sugar and dill, and marinate in plastic wrap so that it will cook itself (they'll have the resultant gravlax for an appetizer); and a medley of scallops, shrimp, and smoked salmon, which he will do up in squid ink pasta, along with red pepper slices, as an accompaniment to the duck. Into a massive teak salad bowl he presses out several garlic cloves, then mixes the paste with the anchovies, along with Worcestershire sauce, lemon juice, mustard, capers, and hot sauce. He tastes his efforts with a spoon and makes an extravagant gesture of approval for Hadley, kissing his fingers with a moue of his lips. The Caesar will have a good scald on it, he tells his daughter. The counter is awash in body parts, spilled sugar, chopped dill, empty sauce bottles, bottle caps, wet spoons, and flour from the sourdough bread. He kneads the bread in a baking bowl, trying to camouflage into the dough the inadvertent smears of blood leaking from the wet kitchen towel around his hand. Jack comes into the kitchen, looks at the carnage on the counter.

"Ew, yuck, Dad. What are you making?" he asks.

"Don't ask," says Hadley.

Charles feels almost happy now—or a state as close

to happy as he has been able to achieve in this house, in this town. If he keeps moving, he is certain, his dinner will be a success. He has to choreograph his pots, conduct the play between the stovetop and the oven so that the ducks won't conflict with the sourdough bread, so that his largest pot will be free for the mussels after he has made the pasta. He doesn't worry much about timing, however: Though his timing in love and finance have been appalling, he has been blessed with an uncanny sixth sense when it comes to cooking. Cooking is orchestral, he decides, resembling something of a symphony or at least a concerto, the movements allegro or largo, depending on the tempo of his swoops and turns as he reaches between the island and the fridge, between the stove and the counter, as he plays the butter of a roux, the garlic of a sauce. He has Bing on now. Can't make a Christmas dinner without Bing, he says to his younger daughter, Anna, who has come into the kitchen to observe the performance. He reaches up to pour himself another tumbler of the Kendall-Jackson, a nice dry red, which he opened because he needed it as the finishing touch to the marinade, and as he does so he notices that the bottle is nearly empty. His dress shirt and the pants to his suit are spotted with olive oil and flour and bits of something brown that might be blood. He has an apron somewhere in the kitchen, but he has been unable to find it.

Outside the warm kitchen, a gust of rain sweeps against the windows, rattling the windowpanes. He takes a sip of the dregs of the red, looks through the panes to the sheets of water beyond. He wonders where she is, what she is doing at this precise moment. He glances at the phone, thinks fleetingly of calling her, then shakes off the desire: He cannot risk hearing the resonant voice of her husband, having to hang up on the man once again. He tries to imagine what her husband looks like, tries to envision the body that might go with the voice; Charles has never asked Siân, and she has not volunteered any details, about her husband's appearance. With the heel of his hand, he punches down the rising dough in the bread bowl, pummels it roughly. He wants her now, with an ache that is not physical, or not entirely physical. His body feels taut, stretched with wanting her, wanting simply to be in her presence. He bends suddenly at the waist, touching his forehead to the surface of the island. He wants to lower himself to the floor. His insides feel hollow, empty without her.

"Daddy?"

Charles glances up quickly, remembers his children. Hadley looks quizzical.

He forces himself upright, smiles.

"Dessert," he says.

"Dessert?"

"I have to think about dessert."

"I want Christmas cookies," says Anna.

He opens a cookbook on the island. He contemplates the ceiling. Winston, who has come to him, nuzzles his knees. He has an image of a French tart; no, of a flan. He thinks about custard; does he have the ingredients? He could do a crème brûlée possibly. Yes, that's it, he decides, cracking open another bottle of the

Kendall-Jackson. A ginger crème brûlée—the ginger will be a perfect holiday nuance for the end of the meal. What will he need? he wonders. Eggs? Cream? He has fresh ginger from the marinade. Sugar, of course. And a blowtorch. Can't caramelize the top without a blowtorch. He tries to think where it was he learned this: in the kitchen of a restaurant just outside Providence. He'd inquired of the waiter, as he sometimes did in restaurants, how a dish was prepared (in this case, a particularly fragile peach crème brûlée) and had been summoned into the kitchen by the chef himself, who'd demonstrated the blowtorch technique: Sprinkle a thin layer of granulated sugar along the top of the custard; blast it with the torch. The process—definitely overkill and probably not ecologically sound—was repeated until the top of the crème was a paper-thin disk of caramelized sugar, like a perfect circle of delicate brown ice.

He gathers on the island the eggs and cream and sugar and ginger, finds a clean bowl and the eggbeater. He stands on a stool, investigates the top shelf of the cabinet over the fridge. He has an idea that there is behind the champagne glasses a set of custard dishes, ramekins, perfect for the crème brûlée. He sees them, snakes his hand through the champagne glasses, then hears his name spoken by his wife in a tone that reminds him of a teacher he had in seventh grade.

"Charles."

He teeters for a moment on the stool, turns around to face his family. They are standing there beneath him, aligned at the end of the counter—Harriet, Hadley,

Jack, and Anna. The tableau they make is characterized by composite alarm. He knows how he must look to them—the singular embodiment of the chaos he has created, both within the kitchen and without. He holds a champagne glass in one hand, a ramekin in the other. His shirt is soaked under the armpits, smeared with duck entrails and flour; the kitchen towel is still ineffectually wrapped around a hand. They stare at him as if at any moment he might be able to explain himself. From his considerable height, he surveys the kitchen—a bloody and ungentle mess, a manic attempt to stave off the unbearable sadness of Christmas.

He looks at his children and his wife, at the walls of a house he no longer owns.

"No one is saved, and no one is totally lost," he tells his assembled family.

*T*he sun had set not a half hour before, and in the west there was still an orange dust at the horizon. The air was dry, the evening lit up already with the summer constellations. He walked her down with the others to the water's edge, where tonight there would be a bonfire, a small celebration for the Fourth. In his hand he carried sparklers. He gave one to her, lit it for her with the matches he had in his shirt pocket. The golden sprinkles from the sparklers illuminated their faces. In front of them, and behind them, there was laughter and chatter, as the others walked singly or in pairs, some with sparklers of their own. It was exciting, this walk in the darkness down to the lake, the path known but not certain, the event producing in the air a sense of freedom, an element of risk.

The counselors had made the pyre already, were hovering importantly nearby. The children took their places in a semi-circle around the wood and the straw, facing the lake. It was the last night of camp, and friendships had formed, delineated in the shapes that drew closer to each other. She sat beside him on the ground, their knees raised, their arms touching from the shoulder to the elbow, and for a time it was all that she could absorb—the length and dizziness of that touch, a thin delicate line along her skin. Until he moved his arm and put it around her, finding with his fingers first the capped sleeve of her blouse, then the skin beneath it. Neither spoke or dared to look at the other.

The straw was lit, bursting noisily into flames, crackling toward the sky, letting loose a shower of sparks that arced upward and died before they could fall on hair and bare skin. Someone, a figure lit by the fire, led the group in songs, summer camp songs and songs for the Fourth. The boy sang beside her, his voice nearly a man's, but she could not sing. She felt the pressure of his arm along her back, the imprint of his fingers on her skin. The fire obscured the cross, obliterated the lake.

When the singing was over, the counselors produced long sticks and marshmallows. The boy hesitated, moved his arm away from her, stood up. She watched him walk toward the counselors, take a stick and a marshmallow, poke it toward the fire, which had settled some. She watched his back, his body just a silhouette. He spoke to another boy.

He returned, sat facing her. He removed the gooey marshmallow, charred on the outside, and held it out to her. She exclaimed, started to speak, so that when he thrust it toward her, it caught on her lips and teeth, smearing her mouth. In the confusion, laughing at the mess, she licked the marshmallow from his fingers as he tried to push it in. She caught one finger between her teeth, released it. Embarrassed, she laughed again and said that he was mean.

He licked the stickiness from his own fingers. When they were clean, he put his hand into his pocket and withdrew an object. She couldn't see in the darkness what the object was. He held it for a moment, then seized her arm at the wrist. He put the object into her palm, closing his hand for a moment over hers. She fingered the object, rolled it in her palm. She felt the links of a chain, the sharp edges of metal charms.

"It's a bracelet," she said, holding it in a fist. Her breath was tight and shallow.

"I wanted something to give you," he said beside her.

When she looked at him, she could see only that half of his face that was lit by the orange of the fire, a light that made shadows in his eyes and with his cheekbones.

He took her hand, and she thought that he might remove the bracelet from her fist and put it on her, but instead he made her stand up. He led her up the path, away from the others; the chatter and the laughter around the bonfire faded as they walked. Above them, trees rustled in the night breeze. In the distance, up the hill, she could see the glow of the lights in the main house, the lights from the dining room, some individual lights in the bedrooms where they had been left on.

When they were halfway up the path, the boy

stepped off the worn track and into the woods. She was not sure exactly what he meant to do, but strangely, she was not afraid. She followed closely behind him, sometimes touching his shirt, as he led the way, held branches for her, pointed out to her where there was a rock or a log. She wondered briefly how they would find the path again, then dismissed her worry. All she could think was that within hours her parents would come to the camp to fetch her and drive her north to Springfield, and that she might never see this boy again.

An owl hooted, startling them both. She laughed nervously, reached out for him. He stopped, turned to face her. She could barely see his eyes in the moonlight, the strong moonlight that had been on the path obscured now by the overhead trees. She sensed rather than saw him, felt his presence near, his own shallow breathing, the heat from his chest and arms. "The stars are amazing tonight," he said, looking up at the sky. "Can you read the constellations?"

"The Big Dipper," she said. "And sometimes the Little Dipper. But that's all."

"Mmmm. Me too." He took a step closer, so that his face was just over hers.

He tilted his head slightly, bent to kiss her. Instinctively she raised her chin. He caught her at the side of the mouth, held his lips there. The kiss was dry and feathery, so tentative she was not certain they were actually touching, though she could feel his breath on her cheek. He put his hands on her arms; she lifted her hands so they touched his back. She had never kissed a boy before, had never even held hands with a boy until she met him. Each touch was new and exhilarating, but she knew that he would not hurt her.

He found her mouth, the whole of it, and drew her in to him with his hands at the back of her waist, so that she lost her balance, was leaning against him for support. He swayed with her weight, then together they knelt. He lost his own balance then and carried her onto the soft mulch of the forest floor. Lying that way, as if on a bed, they became aware simultaneously of what it was they were doing. He pulled his face away to look at her in the dim light, to see if there was alarm there, if he had transgressed. She returned his gaze, but she could not speak. He kissed her once more, not so tentatively this time, and she felt something of his urgency, her own awkwardness. He kissed her for a long time, and there was again the fluttering in her abdomen. His hand moved along her rib cage. She thought that possibly she should move his hand away; it was what she had been taught. He touched her breast, enclosed it with his palm. The touch caught her breath; the fluttering sensation spread out from her abdomen and along her thighs like the spill of a warm liquid. He looked down at her breast, to where her nipple was hard against the cotton of her blouse. She could hear his breathing, faster now, like her own, a rhythm against her face and in her ear. He kissed the side of her face. She unfastened the top button of her blouse, then the next. He pushed aside the cotton fabric, exposing her breast to the night. He touched the skin with his fingers, delicately and gently, as if caressing something fine and fragile—a spun-glass ornament, or the face of a newborn. He kissed her again on her mouth. She could feel him shift his body, move a leg over hers. He raised his face up, looked again at her eyes. He looked at her breast, lowered his mouth, touched the skin of her breast with his lips. She felt him press against her. Her leg was between his; his between hers. The fluttering deep inside her became a pressure, an exquisite urgency. He put his mouth on her nipple, opened his mouth, and sucked her. She moaned faintly with this pleasure, whispered his name. She felt the urgency burst inside her, spread through her and along her legs. She felt the boy shudder against her, a tight helpless shuddering, her nipple still caught in his mouth. He said her name sharply, pressed his forehead hard against her breastbone.

In her fist, she still held the bracelet.

They lay on the dirt and mulch without moving for a long time, long enough for the moon to shift slightly overhead and shine down upon them through a gap in the leaves. The white fabric of her blouse was blue in the moonlight, and she could see clearly now the length of the boy, from the top of his head, where it rested on her chest, to his feet. As they lay there they could hear the voices of the others, moving up the path to the house, young silvery voices laughing in the darkness not fifty feet from them. She thought then that they ought to try to make their way back, so that they would have the voices to guide them, but she did not want to disturb the boy. When after a time he looked up at her, she saw that his eyes were wet, that he had been crying.

"It's all right, Cal," she said.

He covered her breast with her blouse, buttoned it for her. He lifted himself up, knelt beside her in the piney mulch. He saw her clenched fist. He opened her fingers, took the bracelet, fastened it on her wrist. She sat up, slid the bracelet along her arm.

"What we did . . . ," he said.

She touched the bracelet. "I'm all right, Cal," she said. "It's all right."

"I've never . . ."

"I know."

"Do you understand . . . ?"

She looked down at the bracelet, dangling from her thin wrist. "I'm not sure, but I think so," she said.

"I'm not sorry," he said.

"No. I know," she said. "How could we be?"

He helped her to her feet. Together they brushed bits of bark and leaves from her back, her shorts. They would be in trouble when they returned, required to say where they had been, but that seemed unimportant, meaningless.

"We'll just say we went for a walk, lost track of the time," he said. "They won't like it, but we'd probably both better have the same story."

She nodded. He walked in front of her, held branches for her till he had found the way back to the path. They held hands as they climbed the hill, their footsteps reluctant and slow. At the main door of the house, the door that would admit them to the bright

light of the hall, to the stern queries of their counselors, to their separate wings and separate beds, they
paused. He kissed her quickly on the cheek, lest anyone was watching them.

"I won't be able to say goodbye to you," she said.

THE RAIN HAS STOPPED. THE NIGHT IS STILL. A HUSH EN-velops the house, both inside and out, and except for the occasional whine of the refrigerator or the rumble and whomp of the furnace, all is quiet. He holds in his hand a glass of warm champagne, which he poured from the dregs of a bottle on the kitchen counter. Harriet and his children are in bed. He has no clear idea what time it is; he took his watch off to scour the pots, cannot remember where he put it. He thinks it must be after two o'clock. His parents returned from midnight mass nearly an hour ago with Hadley, asleep on her feet as she stumbled to her room. Harriet has already filled the stockings, cleaned up the bits of crumpled wrapping from the adults' presents, set out the children's gifts under the tree. For Christmas Charles gave his wife an astonishingly tiny video cam-era that the salesman promised would not only be easy to use but also take brilliant movies of his children, an enterprise that now fills Charles with sadness and re-morse. Harriet gave Charles two season tickets to the Red Sox, games he already knows he will never attend. In another life (*what* other life? he asks himself—*this* is his life) he'd have loved the tickets, would have taken Hadley and Jack; the tickets would have framed his summer, would have given him something to look forward to, a way to punctuate the long, hot weeks. But now he feels only a vague sense of loss, as of having misplaced one's childhood.

(He thinks, oddly, of the O. Henry story about the couple who buy each other presents they can no longer use, because of what they've sacrificed to afford the gifts. Might he have used the camera to take movies of the kids at the Red Sox games? Without the games, or any similar outings, will Harriet want to take movies at all?)

He finishes the warm champagne, sets the glass on the counter. He has had an extraordinary amount of al-cohol to drink today, and yet he has not felt high or drunk or even buzzed. He has been drinking to anes-thetize himself, he knows, an exhausting and futile ef-fort. He walks through the living room, observes the classic picture: the stockings at the mantel, the pres-ents arranged artfully under the tree. Only Anna this year believes in the miracle of a white-bearded man who visits every house in the universe with presents on this one particular night. He realizes with a pang that he doesn't even know what is in the brightly wrapped packages. He has not bought a single gift for any of his children, a ritual that in the past used to give him pleasure. In a few hours, his kids will be awake and demanding that he and Harriet join them downstairs to see what Santa has brought. If he doesn't go up to bed now, he'll get no sleep at all.

The room in which he and his wife share a bed is at the front of the house. White gauze curtains cover the windows, letting in only a pale glaze of light from a streetlamp across the road. The dark shape in the bed is unmoving; he is certain she must be asleep. At dinner, Harriet was cordial but not animated. He thought she seemed preoccupied, distracted, possibly annoyed by the dinner, which, in the end, did not really work as a whole. The children barely ate anything apart from the duck. The others seemed confused by the menu, as though presented with a puzzle in which certain key pieces were missing. The crème brûlée was a hit, however, and he felt inordinately pleased with this finale—the delicate sugar crust flambéed to translucent perfection.

He removes his sweater, a clean shirt he changed into before the relatives came, his shoes and socks and slacks. In his underpants, he slips under the heavy quilt, a practiced and delicate movement that disturbs the covers as little as possible, the movements of a thief stealing into a house undetected, the movements of a man who does not want to engage his wife. He knows instantly, however, that he has been heard. When he holds his breath and listens intently, he cannot hear his wife breathing, as he ought to. He turns slowly so that his back is to her, so that he might, with luck, fall asleep at once, but as he does, he feels the covers tug and pull, hears her turn in his direction. A hand is at his back, moving up to his shoulder. He turns his head, but not yet his body.

"Harriet?"

She pulls gently at his shoulder, asking him to face her, a request he cannot deny. He rolls over, his head on the pillow, and looks at her. Her face is grave, as he knows his must be to her. They examine each other in this way for what seems like minutes. She does not speak, but he knows that she will.

"Harriet, what is it?"

She says quietly in the thin artificial light, a light in which he can barely make out the expression in her eyes, "I want you to make love to me."

He opens his mouth to protest, to say, reasonably, that it's after two in the morning and they will have to be up at dawn, to say that he's exhausted after all that cooking. To say that he'll make her come, or rub her back. But he knows he cannot say any of those things, that his voice alone will give him away, will announce that he has betrayed her. Instead he draws her to him, embraces her tightly.

"I've been waiting for you," she says, the words muffled into his chest, and he understands instantly that she means more than just this night.

"Oh, Harriet," he says.

And there is no help for him now. He begins to cry. He holds himself still, not breathing, so that she won't detect his tears, holding the ache deep in his chest and in his throat, but she has known him too long, knows the context of every sigh, of this stiffening of his body.

She pushes herself away, studies him. She seems alarmed now, even more alarmed than she appeared to be in the kitchen earlier.

"Charles, for God's sake, what is it?"

He rolls onto his back, his arms out, looks up at the ceiling. The tears leak out of the corners of his eyes, trail down his cheeks. He knows by the tone in her voice that she will not let this go. He knows, too, that he cannot lie to her, not now.

"I have something to tell you that's going to make you sick," he says.

She sits up abruptly, kneels on the bed facing him. Her bare arms are white in the dim light. He winces as he sees for the first time that she has worn her black silk nightgown, a revealing nightgown with lace at the breasts, which she wears when she wants him to make love to her.

He cannot say what he has to say from a supine position. He sits up, puts on his shirt.

"Where are you going?" his wife asks quickly.

"I'm not going anywhere. I'm just putting on my shirt. I'm cold."

"What is it? What is this thing you have to tell me?"

He buttons his shirt, sits on the edge of the bed, half facing her, half turned away.

"I'm in love with another woman," he says.

He waits for the ceiling to fall, for a tree to smash against the windowpanes. He has been imagining these words, cannot hear even his voice saying them without also hearing a crash of cymbals, the pounding of timpani. The silence then, the absolute silence of the bedroom, astounds him. He is afraid for a moment that he did not actually say the words, that he will have to repeat them, louder this time.

But he hears a sharp intake of breath, sees Harriet's hand rise to her mouth.

"Oh my God," she says.

"Harriet, I'm so sorry. I never meant for this to happen." He shuts his eyes, appalled at the sound of his own voice. The words are offensively trite, each syllable a lie. Of course he meant for this to happen. He *made* it happen.

"I'm going to leave you," he says, more honestly. "I'm in love, and I'm going to leave you."

He dares to look at her now, at the shock on her face. He, too, is stunned by his words, by the baldness of them, by their incontrovertibility. He cannot take them back, should not take them back. He does not want to hurt his wife, but he has to make her understand that this is not casual.

"What are you saying? Who is she?"

"She isn't anyone you know. She lives very far from here."

"Then how do you know her?"

"I met her thirty-one years ago. We spent a week together at camp when we were fourteen, thirty-one years ago."

"You spent one week together thirty-one years ago and you love her?" she asks incredulously. "Or have you known her all along?"

"No. No. No. I just remet her a few weeks ago."

"A few weeks ago?" He hears the bewilderment in his wife's voice, knows how truly mad this must sound.

"Have you slept with her?"

It is, of course, *the* question, the one he has anticipated, dreaded. He hesitates. He will not lie. "Yes," he says.

He hears the moan, the single note of pure pain in his wife's voice.

"How many times?" she asks bravely.

"Not many," he says. "Four times."

"Four times?" she asks incredulously. "You've been with her four times? When? When were you with her?"

"Harriet, does it matter when?"

"I trusted you," she says, loudly now. He cannot ask her not to shout, not to wake up the children. It is her right. He realizes with horror that of course he should not have done this now, not on Christmas Eve, not when the children are in the house, not when they will wake up soon, anticipating the stockings and the presents, and will find what instead—a mother devastated? Harriet slips off the bed, stands up. She shivers in her nightgown. He, too, stands up, reaches for her bathrobe on a hook at the back of the door, hands it to her. She bats it away to the floor.

"I love her," he says, as if to explain. "I always have loved her. We were lovers, even as children, all those years ago."

"And what about me? I thought you loved me."

"I do," he says, "but it's different."

"What's different?"

"It's just different." He hears the evasiveness in his

own voice, but he knows he will never tell his wife that it's different because he never really loved her, because he believes that he and Siân were meant to be mates. This is the worst heresy, not something that Harriet ever needs to know.

"Is she married?"

"Yes."

"And does she have children?"

"Yes. She has one, a girl. She had a boy, but he died when he was nine."

"And you're going to be a father to someone else's child?" This last is said in a high-pitched wail, as though this, more than any other betrayal, hurts most. She flails out at him with her fists held together, like a tennis player grasping a racket for a tough backhand shot. She hits him in the rib cage. He holds his arms aloft, does not stop her. She hits him again, and then again. She whacks him a fourth time, then whirls around, sobbing.

"How could you?" she cries.

He cannot tell her why. The why is clear and not clear, as simple as animals mating, or as complicated as a physics problem—a labyrinthine equation of time and distance.

She falls back onto the bed, puts her hands over her face. He cannot tell whether or not she is crying; he thinks she may still be too stunned for tears. He reaches down on the floor for his pants, puts them on, buckles the belt. Hearing the clink of metal on metal, Harriet takes her hands away from her face, watches him dress himself.

"Where are you going?" she asks quietly from the bed.

"I don't know," he says. "I can't stay here now. Not tonight."

"But the children. It's Christmas tomorrow."

The realization seems to strike her even as she announces the import of the morning to her husband. She twists her head and moans again, a terrible, plaintive sound that he has never heard before from his wife, not even when she was in labor with Hadley, the worst of them. Harriet throws an arm across her face, covering her eyes.

Charles looks at his wife on the bed, at the black silk nightgown on the white sheet, at his wife's breasts, small and flat under the open lace. It is conceivably the last time he will ever see his wife's body. No, he thinks again: It is positively the last time he will ever see her body. A body that he has made love to thousands of times. A body that carried and bore and nursed his three children.

"I'll come back," he says. "Before the kids are up. I'll spend the night, or what's left of it, someplace, maybe a motel, and then I'll come back to be with them when they open their presents. We'll tell them together, tomorrow night or the next day."

She lies still on the bed, her face shielded. He thinks she will not speak, that she acquiesces with her silence, as bewildered on this foreign territory as he is. But then she sits up sharply, facing him. Her mouth is tight, a thin line of anger. There are vertical lines above her upper lip that he has never seen before.

"Don't you dare to come back here," she says evenly. "Don't you come back here ever. You want your things, you can send someone else for them. Or I'll put them out on the street. This is my house now, and you are not to come here again." She turns her head away, puts a hand protectively across her stomach—an unconscious gesture she used to make when she was pregnant.

"But, Harriet, the house . . ."

As soon as he has said the words, he knows he has made an unforgivable mistake. She twists quickly around, poised for more pain. He can see it on her face, in the fear in her eyes. It was her mentioning the house that caused him foolishly to blurt out the one thing he has not intended to tell her yet, certainly not on this night. His mind leaps, somersaults. He tries desperately to think of how to extricate himself.

"What?" she says anxiously. "What?"

"Harriet . . ."

"What?" she cries. She turns, springs off the bed. She faces him, her arms locked across her chest. "What?" she cries again, defiantly.

"Harriet, I feel sick about this. You can't know how bad I feel about this. . . ."

"For God's sake, spit it out," she screams. "We've lost the house, haven't we?"

He walks around to her side of the bed, extends his arms to embrace her. For a moment, she lets him, leans into him.

"How could you . . . ?" she asks. "How long have you known this was coming?"

"I've known for a while," he says. "But I just found out for certain this morning. I was at the bank."

She sits down abruptly upon the bed, as if she has fallen.

"I'll take care of you, Harriet," he says. "I'll always take care of you and the children. And they've got to give us at least sixty days before they foreclose. Perhaps . . ."

"I'm going downstairs," she says, almost in a whisper. "I'm going to sit down there until you're gone. Don't be long, because I'm very, very tired."

She stands, walks slowly to the other side of the bed, bends to the floor, and retrieves her robe. She slips her arms through the sleeves, wraps the robe tightly across her chest, securing it with the sash, as though she realized she was exposed, does not want him to see her skin.

Charles watches Harriet leave their bedroom, shutting the door behind her.

He stands for a time in the center of the room, staring at the shut door. Numbly, he turns, puts on his shoes and socks. He takes a jacket from a hanger in the closet. From the drawers of his bureau, he makes a pile of socks and underwear and ties and shirts. He is barely aware of what he is collecting; he simply wants to make a pile. He slips another suit jacket from a hanger, wraps the untidy bundle in the jacket, knots the bundle with the sleeves of the jacket, puts the bundle under his arm. He does not look again at the bed, or at the bedroom that he has shared with his wife for sixteen years. He opens the door, listens intently for sounds in the hallway. He passes the rooms where his children are sleeping, knows he cannot bear to look at Jack in his bed, instead opens the door to Hadley's room. He sees her head on her pillow, her brown hair spread out behind her. Her eyes are open—watchful brown eyes, so like his own.

"Where are you going?" she asks from the bed. He thinks he hears a tremor in her voice. He does not know what she has heard.

"I'm not going far," he says.

He walks to the bed, sits at the edge. He smooths her hair with his hand.

"What's wrong, Daddy? You look so sad."

She sleeps on a pillow with a white lace ruffle; she cradles in her arm a worn and threadbare pink giraffe, a relic of her childhood.

He cannot tell his daughter he is leaving her. His throat feels swollen, suffused with its ache.

"I'm not sad," he tells his daughter. "You'd better try and get some sleep. Morning will be here before you know it."

Hadley dutifully closes her eyes. His daughter, unlike his wife, will not ask to hear what she knows she cannot yet absorb. His daughter will wish away the voices behind the closed door, may come to believe by morning that they were only voices in a bad dream.

He kisses his daughter at the side of her face.

Holding his bundle, he descends the stairs, walks through the silent house. He finds his overcoat on the clothes tree, his car keys on the counter. Through the door of the family room, he sees his wife—a small, huddled shape on a couch. She is looking at her palms, which are resting on her knees, as if she were trying to read there what has happened to her, what will happen to her.

He says, "I'll be back before the kids are up."

She does not acknowledge this promise. He opens the door, leaves his house and family behind him.

*A*nd what can you say about a soiled shirt, a shirt that does not belong to your husband, hiding in your drawer?

He held it in his hands like evidence.

I said, my voice no more than a whisper, that I had taken the shirt from my father's laundry basket the last time I was visiting, that I had planned to knit a sweater for him for Christmas.

Stephen might have said, The size is wrong.

And I'd have had to lie again.

But he didn't. What was the point?

I remember that he sat down at the place where he had been, at his place within the family, near the fire. His eyes were inward, closed to me. My hands shook. I couldn't stop them. I hadn't meant for this to happen. But if I hadn't meant for this to happen, why had I kept the shirt?

I remember, too, that I was afraid. It was a kind of

fear that I had never felt before: a sense that glass would shatter, cutting each of us.

I had to go upstairs to get the gift for Lily. Stephen had forgotten to bring it down.

Lily felt the tension in the air. Looked at me and then her father.

The relatives came for the meal. They seemed, with their broad smiles and appetites, bright cartoon figures entering suddenly a darkened film—characters misplaced or lost. Or was it we who were misplaced, had lost our place?

I served the food that I had made. I smiled, said pleasant things. I could do this, had to do this for Lily, had to serve as a foil for Stephen, who could barely eat. From time to time I looked at his face, and it was white, preternaturally colorless. I thought to myself: How can I have done this to any man? And then I thought: Why, in choosing you, did it have to be something I had done to Stephen? What was the contract that Stephen and I had made? Where did it begin or end?

After the meal, the children dispersed to reinspect their toys. We were invited to go to Stephen's brother's house for dessert, as was the custom. I said yes too quickly. I wanted to be out of my house, away from the fear. I had set something in motion, and I did not yet know how it would play out. I wanted, too, to be away from the phone hanging quietly upon the wall. I thought that you might call, was more afraid that I would.

I bundled Lily up in her coat. I put my scarf on, then

my boots. I looked at Stephen, who was not dressed for the cold.

You go on with the rest, he said, not looking at me. I think I'm getting another migraine. I'll just lie down, come along in an hour or so.

I did not believe him about the migraine, but I understood that he needed to be alone. I thought briefly that he might go looking for other evidence, the letters and the package that he now must be wondering about. I thought that now I should stay—but there was Stephen's brother waiting for us by the door, waiting to take Lily and me to his house so that Stephen could follow in our car later.

I hesitated, put my hand on Stephen's sleeve. You rest, I said. Come if you can. When I get home, we'll talk.

He turned away, said nothing. I looked quickly at Stephen's brother, who had heard.

The phone rang. I was paralyzed. Stephen glanced at the phone, looked at me. I walked to the phone. When I picked it up, my hand shook so badly I was afraid I might drop the receiver. I said, tentatively, Hello, praying it wasn't you. It was my father, wishing us all a merry Christmas. My relief was sharp, and I began to cry. I turned my back to the kitchen so the others wouldn't see.

In Stephen's brother's house, I saw blurred shapes and scenes, rushes from a film that was playing on furniture and faces, strange distorted limbs, bodies wrapped around an armchair, moving soundlessly against the shiny metal of a toaster or a teapot.

I hoped that Stephen was sleeping, knew that he was not. I did not know if he was opening drawers in his office, or pacing in the bedroom.

An hour passed and then another. I went to the telephone, called my house. There was no answer. I sat back down at the table.

I knew then. It was a feeling that came on like a chill, first along the hairs of my arm, then along my spine, and settling finally at the back of my neck.

I stood up, reached for my coat.

Keep Lily here, I said to Stephen's brother.

HE SLOWS THE CADILLAC WHERE THE TARMAC MEETS THE wood, wary of ice that may have formed on the bridge during the earlier storm. The night is still and dark, the visibility poor, no moon yet to delineate the bridge's span above the water. Beside him on the seat is the bundle of clothes. He is now, in all senses of the word, homeless—an alien and yet oddly comforting sensation, a state of being that seemed heightened during his solitary drive down High Street, his the only vehicle on the road, the windows of the houses he passed shuttered and closed to him.

He knows exactly where she is right now, exactly what she must be doing: lying in a bed next to her husband, waiting for her daughter to wake up. He knows he tortures himself with images of Siân with her husband, like a masochist poking a sore tooth, but he hopes that somehow if he looks at the images enough, forces himself over and over to examine them, he might finally be able to absorb them, diffuse their power. On his way to the bridge, he passed half a dozen phone booths he knows well, slowed the car at each, thinking momentarily that he might impulsively call her despite the idiocy of the hour, had to will himself not to stop the car. He wants, needs, to hear her voice—to make the connection of now-familiar sound waves across a wire. He wants to call her to tell her what he has done, to tell her simply that he is not sleeping in a bed with someone else, will never do so again.

He parks in the middle of the bridge, halfway along its length. He emerges from the car, walks to the railing. Underfoot he feels a splintered board, a sliver missing. In good weather, walking across the bridge, one can see through the slats the water below, the shallow green water where the bridge meets the beach, the deep navy of the channel. When he takes that walk, and even when he drives the bridge's span, he often thinks of the pilings beneath the bay, of the force of the tides against the thick round wooden columns. He wonders how the engineers who maintain the bridge know when the pilings need replacing, how it is that their concrete anchors never seem to shift in the sand, causing a sudden give in the planking.

He feels rather than sees the rough surface of the railing. He remembers the first day that he touched Siân, on the bench, bringing his lips to her nipple, not knowing as he did so what was happening, what he was making happen. He had wanted a return to innocence. He remembers, too, the last time he lay with Siân, the last time they made love, how they both fell into a deep, seamless sleep, even though it was morning, how when he awoke he still had his finger inside her, and how he realized that for that to have occurred, neither one of them must have stirred even a fraction while they slept. Was there, or could there ever be, he wondered then, and wonders now, a reconciliation between innocence and sexuality?

A breeze drifts along the length of the bridge; below him he can hear the slap of waves. He cannot see much: a hint of land where there are lights at the shoreline. He looks over toward the east, where the sun will rise soon, where the dunes and the spit meet the other end of the bridge. In Portugal it's already Christmas morning, has been for some time. He knows little about how the Portuguese celebrate this holiday, other than that they must. He doesn't know much about Portugal at all actually, except for its food, or at least those dishes that have made their way across the Atlantic. He wonders when exactly he will ever get to Portugal: He cannot imagine traveling there alone now.

He raises his collar, leans on his elbows. He bends his head, shuts his eyes. He knows he should ask for forgiveness, that what he has done to Harriet and his children is reprehensible, that his wife is still probably sitting on the couch trying to comprehend the scope of this betrayal.

He turns around, rests his back against the railing. His coat falls open; he lifts his head to the sky, searching for a star. He wants to reach across a lifetime, to reclaim what once was forfeited.

In the overcast sky, he cannot find a star. He pulls

his coat to, knows he needs a room now, if only for a few hours. He tries to think where there might be a motel open this time of year, winces as he imagines the thoughts of the night manager booking in a man alone on Christmas.

He walks to the car. He hears the clock tower ring three bells.

He remembers when there were prayers for different dilemmas.

*T*he light was blinding on the surface of the snow, a painful light you wanted to ward off with your hands. I turned too quickly into the drive, skidded on the ice. The car thudded softly into the snowbank that Stephen's brother had made when he'd plowed the drive before the meal was served. I left the car door open, ran up the stairs to the kitchen. I called his name—once, twice, three times—and heard no answer. I thought he might be in the barn, did not want to think of what I might find there. I turned then and saw through the window that the barn door was open.

I left the house and walked quickly to the barn. The building was old, with wide plank siding, and sometimes in the winter, if the air was dry, the boards contracted, pulled away from each other, leaving thin seams of air and light from without or within. I hesitated at the barn's entrance, looked through a crack

in the wall. I saw the ocher flannel shirt, a dark red
stain.

I ran to where Stephen was sitting on an old wooden
chair he had thought years ago to refinish and had
brought to the barn, where it had remained all that
time. There was a shotgun at his feet. The wound was
to his shoulder; he was holding his arm limply in his
lap. One sleeve was soaked with blood—a drenching,
rusty spill.

He was barely conscious. His hand was already gray
beneath a blotting of the rust.

I said, Stephen.

He looked at me, tilted his head. The pain was visible on his face.

I touched his hand.

I'm so sorry, I said to him.

I watched the paramedics wrap my husband in warm
quilts, tie him to a stretcher, and carry him out into the
overbright sunshine of the yard. Later, the surgeon who
stitched him said that he would lose the use of his arm.
I wondered how it had happened: Had his hand shaken
so badly that he had missed?

I understood that this was not for the shirt, nor for
the onion sets that had been washed away, but for a
life, a way of life, that might have to go with the onion
sets.

I understood that it was for having had the farm at
all. To release him from the farm.

And I understood, too, that it was for the missed
connection—for an emptiness I had failed to fill.

When the paramedics had gone and I had said that

I would follow, I went back into the barn. I scrubbed the chair and the floorboards. I think it strange now that I did not cry. I washed the chair clean, but I could not remove the stain from the wooden floor, from the tiny cracks where the color had settled in.

HE HAS WAITED LONG ENOUGH. YESTERDAY, CHRISTMAS Day, with its excruciating pain and elaborate pretense, was, he thinks, the longest day of his life. After his drive to the beach, he found a motel room at the edge of town, slept until sunlight blurred the edges of the shades, then drove back to his house for the charade of Christmas morning. He found Harriet, ashen-faced, an automaton, a smile frozen on her lips, sitting in a straight-backed chair, as the children, having demolished their stockings, were opening their presents. Only Hadley of his three children, on the floor with an unopened present on her lap, seemed to sense catastrophe in the air. He took off his coat in the kitchen, sat on the couch, and was immediately inundated with the squeals and queries of Anna and Jack, who pushed presents onto his lap, demanding his attention and scrutiny and, more than once, his aid in assembling toys. Normally that was a task he accepted grudgingly as a necessary fact of fatherhood, but yesterday he welcomed the work: It provided a focus, a distraction from the frozen smile.

When the presents had been opened, assembled, and marginally played with, he went into the kitchen and made pancakes—a ritual of Christmas morning that felt hollow this time. At the dining table, Harriet sat unmoving, a fork stabbed into a pancake, as if she were unable to cut it for herself. Even Jack and Anna began to feel the calamity, turning their gaze from mother to father to mother, then over to Hadley, who seemed, as the eldest, the repository of secrets. Catching Harriet's eye, Charles thought to take the ball from her, ease her task, by beginning the talk himself. (How, he had no idea; he had not prepared for this, could not even imagine the vocabulary with which one told a child this terrible thing.) But Harriet, seeing his intent, shook her head quickly. He didn't know if her gesture meant not now, or not today, or not at all, but it wasn't his place to question her, not his decision.

Awkwardly, after the meal, Charles stood in the middle of the family room, dispossessed, unsure of whether or not he had the right even to go upstairs to the bathroom to fetch his toilet kit, which, in his haste the night before, he had left. He had tended the fire, cleaned up the wrappings from the presents, finished the breakfast dishes, and was now unemployed. Normally they'd have gone visiting—to his parents, to her parents, for more food, to see the trees. He supposed that Harriet still planned to make these trips, was unclear if he should accompany her. Ought they to make a clean sweep, telling first the children, then each family—in the way they had once announced the impending birth of Anna?

But Harriet made the decision for him. She said simply, at his side, "Go now."

He turned to her, thinking he would ask her if she didn't want him to stay, to help her tell the children, but her face was impenetrable. She answered for him the unspoken query.

"I'm going to tell them when you're gone," she said.

He left then, said no goodbyes. The children occupied, he slipped out the kitchen door, feeling small and mean. It was the worst crime, he thought, stealing away from one's children.

He'd driven to the motel, locked himself in his room. He'd wanted desperately to call Siân, knew that he could not. They'd made an agreement: They wouldn't call each other on Christmas Day. But what agreements were binding now?

He'd tried to sleep, a futile and restless effort. He'd gotten up from the bed, driven to the Qwik Stop for a six-pack, gone back to the room, drunk the six beers, one after the other. Still he couldn't sleep. There was nowhere to go, no one to call. It was Christmas Day, the one day of the year when everyone was occupied, everyone nestled into a family. And whom would he call if he could? Was there anyone to whom he would tell this story, anyone who could understand what he had done? He did not feel sorry for himself, did not want the companionship or understanding of other men. He wanted only to talk to the one person, hear the one woman's voice. He thought that if he could talk to her, he would be able to sleep. Everything would be all right.

He'd driven to the beach then. Straight across the bridge to the dunes. He'd walked the spit in its entirety, the air clean and chill, the sea gradually becoming rougher than it had been during the hours before dawn. He liked the sun on his face, even though it gave off little warmth. On his way back along the beach, in his crumpled suit and overcoat and soiled shirt, he walked at the edge of the hard sand left by the tide and thought of Winston. And when he thought of Winston, he was immediately mired in the imponderables left in the wake of his pronouncement to his wife: Who would keep Winston now? Himself? His children? And with those questions, immediately there were others: Where would he live in the interim until Siân could get free? Would she want to get free? Where would his wife and children live when the house was foreclosed? How could he keep his business going if the business was located in a house he could no longer enter? Did he have a business left at all? And how was he going to pay for everything?

The questions made him dizzy. Or perhaps it was his hunger. He hadn't eaten anything since the eclectic dinner of Christmas Eve. (Was that really only the night before? he wondered in amazement; it seemed as though days had intervened.) And like Harriet, he had not touched the pancakes at breakfast. It was—he looked around him for the sun—what time now? He minded that he hadn't thought to collect his watch when he was in the house earlier. He thought it must be midafternoon, three o'clock, perhaps later. He'd driven then to a bar outside town where he knew he would not be recognized, had a sandwich there and a couple of beers in the company of the saddest men he thought he had ever seen, and when he'd emerged it was dark. Dark enough so that he could return to the motel and imagine that the day was over, dark enough to wish the day behind him.

He'd slept briefly, woken with a start. He called the motel owner to find out the time, was disheartened to learn that it was only seven-thirty in the evening. He'd driven back then to the Qwik Stop, bought another six-pack along with a toothbrush and a razor and, for good measure, a package of over-the-counter sleeping pills. If he didn't sleep tonight, he thought, he would go mad.

He *had* slept, fitfully, twenty minutes at a time, once waking up in the midst of a nightmare in which his house was floating in the bay and he could see Winston in a lower window, drowning. He'd had another dream, a sort of erotic nightmare, in which he and Siân were making love in his marital bed when Hadley entered the room. He'd woken from this dream with his shirt soaked. He'd sat up quickly, stripped the shirt from his skin, had a shower. In the shower, he determined that it was perhaps better after all not to sleep, spent the rest of the night until dawn sitting in the dark in the only chair in the room, finishing the rest of the beers.

* * *

It is ten minutes to ten now; he knows from the clock in the Cadillac, the clock still keeping accurate time after 140,000 miles. He is parked beside the best-situated phone booth in town, a booth at the back of a small fish market at the end of a pier in the harbor. It is a phone people seldom use, chiefly fishermen calling home to their wives. In the half-dozen times he has called her from here, the only sounds he has had to compete with are the slapping of the waves along the dock, the frenzied cries of gulls looking for chum.

His heart racing, his fingers shaking more from nerves than from lack of sleep, he punches in the digits of her phone number, then his credit card. The phone rings once, twice, three times. He prays fervently and rapidly that her husband is out of the house. He brushes the hair from his forehead, looks around him from habit. The dock is deserted, this day after Christmas.

She answers tentatively, as she almost always does.

"Siân," he says with enormous relief. He is afraid for a moment that he might actually begin to weep with relief.

"Charles."

"I thought I'd go out of my mind if you didn't answer," he says in a rush.

"Oh . . ." Her voice sounds guarded, careful.

"What is it?" he asks. "Is your husband there in the room?"

"No," she says, in a voice she might use to give information to a woman friend, an acquaintance. "My husband's brother is here with his family." She pauses. "Visiting . . . ," she says carefully.

"Siân, listen to me. You don't have to say anything. I'll do the talking. But there's something very important I have to tell you."

"What?"

"I've told my wife."

"What?"

"I've told my wife."

There is a long pause at her end.

"I don't understand."

"I've told my wife that I'm in love with you. That I'm leaving her."

The pause this time is so long he thinks she may have hung up the phone. Finally he hears her say, quietly, under her breath, as if she had turned her head away from the people in the room, "Oh, no." She repeats this—two low, sonorous syllables. "Oh, no."

"It's done."

"No," she says, again quietly. "No."

"Siân, it's done. It's over."

"What happened? Why?" she asks, her voice rising.

"It was awful. Just awful."

"You can't . . . ," she says.

He waits. "What?"

"Listen," she says, her voice barely a whisper. "You have to get it back. You have to talk to her, get her to take you back. You can't have done this. We can't have done this."

"Siân, it's done. I couldn't live that way. I couldn't keep lying, whatever happened. I'm not telling you you have to leave your husband. I'm just telling you what I had to do."

"I know. I know."

"Well, then."

"I can't talk now. Something's happened," she whispers. She says, in a louder voice, "So how was your Christmas?"

"When can I talk to you? When can I call?"

"You can't. Not today. I'll write."

"Write! I'll go out of my mind waiting for a letter. Let me call you later."

"No, you can't. You don't understand." And again, in a louder voice, "Lily is fine."

"OK, OK. But promise me this. You'll write today."

"Yes."

"And send it Express. I'll get it tomorrow."

"Yes."

"And listen, take down this number. It's the motel where I'm staying. Just in case. Call me anytime you can. From a phone booth. Any hour."

"OK."

"Siân, I love you."

"I know."

"I don't want to hang up."

"I know."

"I don't want to let you go."

He hangs up the phone, unable to say goodbye. He picks it up immediately, hears the buzz of the dial tone. He stands with the phone in his hand, unable to move, reluctant to replace the receiver.

He looks out toward the end of the dock, takes a great gulp of air. What could possibly have happened that she needs to tell him about?

He replaces the receiver, walks to his car. He hits the steering wheel with the heel of his hand. There is nothing he can do but wait, a task at which he is remarkably poor. He has all but promised her he will not call her again. He could hear the fear in her voice. Something is very wrong, and she can't tell him what it is.

He puts the car in gear, heads down High Street, thinks of driving west to Pennsylvania. Instead he passes the street on which he used to live, makes the turn. He sees his house; Harriet's station wagon is not there. He takes a chance, pulls the Cadillac into the driveway. He hears no sounds, sees no faces in the windows. When he opens the kitchen door, the silence is complete: Not even Winston is here, bounding out to greet him as he normally would. Charles looks at the disarray in the family room—children's toys strewn about, abandoned. On the counter in the kitchen is a note in Harriet's hand: "We're at my sister's. I don't know when we'll be back."

Charles picks up the note, walks to his study, at the front of the house. Of course he understands why she has left with the children: she cannot bear the house now, a house so full of memories, a house she cannot have. He wonders if he should call, decides he should not, not today anyway. He hasn't planned on coming here, hasn't planned on working, but as long as he is here, he wonders if he oughtn't to try to get something done—something to while away the hours until Harry Noonan opens the post office tomorrow. He could fill some cartons with his papers so that he could sort through them back at the motel. Or perhaps, with Harriet and the children gone, he could work here for a couple of hours, listen to his messages, return the most important calls, get out some mail.

He enters his study, sees immediately another note on his desk. In his coat, he sits in his office chair, picks it up. It is written in purple crayon, on the back of a piece of his business stationery. The handwriting is Jack's.

He crumples the note in his fist, looks out his study window to the yard, where he can see the long rope swing he threw over the walnut for Hadley and the others. In the silence of his study, he opens the note, reads again the childlike scrawl.

The note contains only one word, a question.

Why?

The house was full of people, Stephen's brother and his wife, their children. They were solicitous and guarded. They wanted to ask, but did not, what exactly it was that had caused Stephen to be in the barn with a gun on Christmas Day. Stephen, in the hospital, would not say. Lily was told only that there'd been an accident.

I wrote the letter to you, as you had asked, and put it in the mail. I knew when I wrote it that it was irrevocable, and, when I mailed it, that it was irretrievable. I knew, too, that if a heart can be said to be broken, this letter would break your heart, because it had broken mine. And yet love—the love that we shared so briefly—lodges not in the heart but in the brain, and with the brain there are always thoughts, always memories.

The afternoon I handed the Express Mail package to the woman behind the counter at the post office, it seemed to me that I was giving over to her a great secret, forfeiting a mystery.

The next morning, the house still full of people, I dressed my daughter and put her in the car. We needed milk, cereal, eggs, bread for toast, and coffee. I did not want to think about when your post office would open, about how you would find the red-white-and-blue package, about how you would rip it apart, take it to your car. I did not want to think about your face when you had read the letter.

The A&P was not crowded; some early morning shoppers like myself, looking for their breakfast or thinking to get this chore done early. I put Lily in the basket in the cart, started down the aisles. Overhead was the piped-in music, a lazy drone I barely heard. I put bananas and oranges into the cart, potatoes for dinner. In another aisle, the next, I found cereal and coffee, put them idly in. I opened Lily's coat, I remember, shook open my own. It was hot inside the store; we were overdressed.

In the third aisle, the refrigerator aisle, I saw at its end a worker, a tall boy with pimples, in a white coat, whose task it was that morning to put prices on the orange juice, restack the eggs. I headed down the aisle, picked up a hefty gallon of milk, some yogurt, a container of cottage cheese. I was thinking about whether it would be more economical in the long run, since there were so many people in the house, to purchase cans of frozen orange juice rather than the brand in the carton that I preferred, when I heard the song.

Perhaps a bar or two had passed before it registered,

before it stopped me, there in the middle of the aisle. I listened to its melody, its words, a simple pop song of no consequence to anyone else in the store, yet to me, at that moment, it was a call across the years, a cry across three states.

I began soundlessly to mouth the words. Lily looked up at me and smiled, then stopped smiling when she saw that I was crying. I put sound to the words, a hesitant, cracked sound that was something like singing. The boy, the teenage boy with pimples at the end of the aisle, heard my infelicitous voice, saw me standing paralyzed with my shopping cart in the aisle. Another woman, an older woman with tight gray curls and wearing what we used to call a loden coat, turned the corner into the aisle, looked first at the boy, then at me, to see what was the matter. My voice is terrible; I am not a singer. But I didn't care. What was there to be ashamed of, what was there to lose? I opened my mouth wider. I sang as if I were not normally chagrined by my voice, I sang as if I had wanted to belong to a band all my life, I sang as though the song were a prayer and I a priest, begging for its meaning.

The song—a simple song with enigmatic words and lovely flourishes—finished abruptly, leaving me stranded in the aisle to no applause.

I picked up Lily, abandoned the cart with all that I had put into it. I carried Lily to the front of the store, looked frantically for a phone booth. It was twenty past eight. I had to reach you before you went to the post office. I was crazed, intent. I was crying too—I didn't care. I yelled up to the manager, in his booth above the shoppers, to let me use the phone. He said there was a pay phone just outside the store, around the corner. I ran with Lily past the startled woman at the register, ran past the long line of carts, found the phone booth against the wall. I put Lily down, reached for quarters in the bottom of my pocketbook. Lily started to wander away; I put my leg around her, held her to me. I found the piece of paper in my wallet, punched in numbers, fed the box with quarters as if it were a child you wanted to keep quiet with cookies.

The phone rang. A man answered. I asked for you. He said that there were no phones in the rooms, but he would be glad to give you the message. I told him very carefully what the message was: Don't open the letter. Go directly to The Ridge. I would meet you there.

I made the motel manager repeat the message. I told him it was essential that he give it to you. Essential. He said that he would walk straight over to your room, give it to you now, and that if you weren't there, he would watch for you, give it to you himself, in person, when you returned.

I thanked him, hung up the phone. I put Lily in the car, drove back to the house.

They were all in the kitchen, waiting for their breakfast, astonished I had returned without the milk and coffee. I said Hello and then Excuse me, and I ran upstairs to the attic.

In the attic, in addition to the trunk that had traveled from Springfield to Dakar and back to the farm, there were cardboard cartons of belongings from my father's attic that he had given to me several years before.

The cartons had been placed along a far wall, behind other trunks, other boxes, in a position that had all but guaranteed their never being opened again. But I was on a mission, determined. No trunk was too large, no object insurmountable. I shifted heavy boxes, wedged myself in. I thought for a moment I might not get out. I made my way to the far wall where the cartons were.

When I reached them, I tore open their tops, upended the boxes onto the attic floor. There were showers of school papers and mementos. In one carton, I heard a promising clink. At the carton's bottom was a box of childhood jewelry—ropes of beads, a pin from the National Honor Society, a handful of gaudy rings. And there, tangled with a necklace, green and sticky with a substance that might thirty years ago have been Kool-Aid, I found the bracelet.

I held it in my hand. as if it were an ancient amulet I had excavated, its worth beyond understanding.

I put it on my wrist.

I went quickly downstairs to where the others were gathered. I hugged Lily, told her to stay with Stephen's brother's family. I told Stephen's brother I might be gone most of the day; it was important. Before he could think to protest, I ran out the door to the car.

I drove seventy, eighty miles an hour, hoping you wouldn't get there before me.

The lawns around The Ridge that day were covered in snow, a pristine snow with a crust that had not yet been trampled upon. I was sure that you would come. I remember feeling exhilarated with the knowledge that you would come, that within an hour or two you would be there with me. I did not precisely know how it would work, but I felt somehow that it would. We would talk, we would hold each other, and we would invent a life.

I thought that I would go for a walk around the inn, perhaps down to the lake. Then I went inside, asked the man at the desk, who knew me, if there was still the badminton court I remembered from childhood. He looked surprised, said yes, the court was still there, though not set up now, of course. But I could walk there if I wanted to. I told him I would like that. He gave me directions. It was across the lawn, down to the left. Behind a hedge. A flat grassy field in the summer, with a bench. I'd know it by the stone bench with the carvings, he said.

I walked across the lawn, making virgin footprints in the snow.

I found the hedge, covered with a thick frosting. I found the bench by the field, brushed off the snow with my gloved hands. I sat on the bench.

I looked across the grassy court, now covered with snow. The sun made a billion brilliant specks on the crust.

I looked across the grassy court. It was summer, and we were children.

And it was then, finally, that I could see it all.

A GUST CATCHES THE METAL MOTEL DOOR, SLAMS IT hard on his fingers. Charles winces, retrieves the door, pushes it against the wind, closes it. His topcoat billows out behind him. He bends into the gale, walking quickly to his car. In the parking lot, bits of debris and dust swirl and eddy, sending grit into the air, into his eyes. The ferocity of the wind surprises him, considering the clarity of the day. Overhead, evergreens sway and bend. A freak storm—a blow without the clouds.

He shuts the door, feels the sanctuary of the car, the quiet as well as the calm. He looks at his fingers, the bruised knuckles, the middle finger swelling already. Checking in the rearview mirror, he sees that his hair is wild about his head. He tries to comb it with his fingers. He notices, too, that his eyes are bloodshot—from too much beer, no doubt, but also from an almost superhuman lack of sleep. He cannot remember the last time he slept a whole night through, cannot really remember the last time he slept more than two hours straight. His face feels grainy, stretched, even though he has just shaved.

He puts the car in gear, heads toward the post office. If he has any luck left at all, Noonan will be there already, and more important, the Express Mail letter will have come in. As has happened to him before, he both dreads and hungers for the letter—hunger winning out. The open line of communication between them seems so fragile, particularly now, when he cannot talk to her on the telephone, when she has been so guarded, that he is eager to restore it, no matter what the cost. If he can talk to her, if she can talk to him, if they can be in each other's physical presence, then he truly believes that they will be all right.

He drives through town, the odd storm creating havoc in the streets. Townspeople, bent double, seem blown from open door to open door. Hats, newspapers, paper bags, trash, and Christmas decorations skim along the streets and lodge momentarily in doorways. He comes to a stop at the traffic light, doesn't like the perilous way it is swinging in the stiff blow. Harborside, he can see the water hit the seawall like a firecracker, explode in a spray that drenches everything within twenty feet of the wall—parked cars, hapless pedestrians, phone lines, the backs of shops. The tide is up. Any higher and there'll be serious flooding in a couple of hours. He thinks of the houses smack up against the water along High Street; there'll be anxious home owners there. He wonders if the spit will breach.

Noonan's Trooper is at the post office. *Yes.* If only his

luck will hold, Charles is thinking, the letter will be there.

He opens the door to the main office. Noonan says immediately, "Got a package for you, Callahan. How was your Christmas?"

Charles signs for the letter.

"Fine," he says, relieved that not everyone in town knows yet about the debacle that was his Christmas. "And yours?"

"Oh, the usual," says Noonan. "Too much food, too many relatives."

"Know what you mean," says Charles, holding the Express Mail package against his chest.

A breastplate.

"Watch yourself out there," Noonan calls to Charles's back. "Got a weird storm working itself up the coast."

Charles nods, hurries to his car, his temporary retreat. (He reflects that his car is one of the few havens he has left now, though GMAC in its wisdom will probably want to repossess it; he could total the car, he thinks idly, before they get their hands on it.) He tears open the packet, sees the thin blue envelope inside. More delicately, he opens the envelope, unfolds the letter. Just the sight of her handwriting is somehow deeply reassuring.

He reads the letter through.

He reads it again.

And again.

He holds the letter in his hand, opens his car door, stands up for air. He turns slowly around, lays his head on top of his car. He looks up, starts walking. He completes a large circle within the post office parking lot, still holding the letter in his hand. His stomach feels hollow, as if he had taken a fist. Above him, tree branches whip against a power line. A woman pulls into the parking lot, emerges from her car. Immediately the wind snatches an envelope from her hand. The envelope rises and falls, slides along the tarmac, lodges in a bush at the side. The woman runs in its wake, a comical and ungainly dash. The letter must be important, Charles thinks distractedly.

He walks back to his car, the door still open, a little bell inside dinging to signal that something is amiss. He looks at the letter in his hand, thinks to fold it up, stick it back inside the thin blue envelope. Instead he reaches up to the cloudless sky, lets the letter go. He watches it loop and fall like a kite, skitter along the side of the post office, then disappear behind the back of the building. He thinks for a minute that he ought to run to catch it, that it is, somehow, valuable, a tangible thread to a precious thing he once owned, then he remembers suddenly that he owns nothing now.

He reenters the Cadillac, no longer a sanctuary. He starts the car, pulls out to an intersection. Behind him a driver leans on the horn. Startled, Charles makes a right turn in the intersection, heading south and west toward the motel.

She has written that it is over. Totally, completely, irrevocably over.

She has written that her husband shot himself and will lose the use of his arm.

She has written that she has loved him.

He proceeds down High Street, unaware that he is

even behind the wheel. He has no destination, no urgency at all. He thinks, oddly, that he will never get to Portugal now. He knows this for a certainty, though he is not sure why. He sees her skating in her boots, cannot bear the image, makes it go away. What is he doing? He cannot go back to the motel. Jesus Christ, he thinks, that's the last place he wants to be. He brakes sharply and suddenly, makes a U-turn in the middle of High Street, causing a long squeal of tires as he does so. He drives, nearly blind, out toward the beach.

To his right, along High Street, he is aware of the hammering of the surf. High upon a hill, he sees Lidell's lost Tinkertoy, rusted beams dancing above the town. He sees houses now with their windows boarded up, sandbags along foundation lines. He hopes his children are inside a house somewhere, hopes Harriet has had the sense to pull them in. The biggest danger is from power lines. He himself has seen them snap and fall, crackling along the pavement.

He sees her on a bed, the lovely tilt of her nostrils. He can feel her hand on his skin.

He sees an image he has often in his dreams: the nipples of her breasts bursting through the white cloth of her blouse. He had it when he was a boy, and then later when he met her again, and he had not had it in all the years in between.

He wonders if the dream will go away now.

In Portugal they might one day have sat at a café in the sun, eating braised octopus and Portuguese sausage. He'd have read to her, or she to him. They'd have drunk red wine and gone swimming and then made love.

Simple pleasures.

He ought to have known it was not possible. He ought to have known she wouldn't leave. She had said it, and he had not paid attention. *Neither one of us can help the other, and that's the truth.*

He sees the bridge in the distance, the surf battering the pilings. No fishermen against the railing today. He wonders if the blow could actually knock a man down. He thinks maybe he'll take the Cadillac straight across the bridge, pile it into the dunes, walk back to town and call GMAC, tell them where they can pick up their car.

He hits the bridge too fast. The rattling boards seem to want to shake the Cadillac apart.

The spray is beautiful at the railings. Splendid and theatrical. The sky above the spray is the darkest blue he has ever seen.

He reaches down in front of the passenger seat, snaps a Bud from its plastic ring. He brings the beer between his legs, pops the top. Eight-twenty in the morning. Perhaps his soul is in jeopardy now.

Looking up from the beer, he sees the sheet of ice. A sheet of ice that must have formed in the night from the spray, a sheet of translucent ice across the bridge. He brakes a split second too late and knows it.

He feels the brakes lock, the car skid. The railing gives with ease, splintering into a thousand bits of wood. He sees Siân's face; he hears his daughter's voice. The Cadillac sails in a magnificent arc, a graceful arc, out toward Portugal.

Timing is everything, he thinks.

For the first time in her life, at breakfast, she had not known how to be. Cal had sat beside her, so near, and yet there was a gulf between them. They could not touch, could not even speak, and within hours, she knew, they would never see each other again. All night she had lain awake in her bed, reliving the moments on the forest floor, unsure of their reality. It wasn't possible such a thing had happened to her, and if it had, what did it mean?

She had worn the bracelet. It had risen and fallen on her thin wrist as she moved her hand, a tangible sign that they had been together. She sat beside him, in her shorts and sleeveless blouse, her stomach knotted with memories of the night before, with a kind of bottomless dread of knowing that she had to say goodbye. She knew that he would not kiss her again, would not be able to in the daylight, and she knew that he would not touch her, not as he had the night before. That was over, encapsulated, a memory now—and it would be many years before she would let a boy touch her in that way again.

She said the word "badminton," and she could see that he was grateful. She spoke to him in a low voice so the counselor would not hear, and when she dared to look at Cal, he was smiling.

She left the dining hall with the others, as if she would walk down the path to the outdoor chapel, as if she would attend this last mass with the group. She walked alone so as not to draw attention to herself, and quietly, when the others were engaged, she slipped to the side, walked along the grass to the field where the badminton court was. She expected someone to call out to her, hunched her back a bit in anticipation, but miraculously, no one seemed to notice she had gone. The morning was hot and damp and still, the sun already high in the cloudless sky. Within hours, when the parents had arrived, retrieved their children, and taken them to their separate homes, the day would be a scorcher.

She saw him sitting on the stone bench already, a bench that had earlier intrigued her. One support was a death's head, a ghoulish face with lolling tongue, a face forever frozen in a grimace; the other was a madonna-like figure, except that the young woman, whose breast was bared, carried a stone rose, not a child. The boys tittered at the figure when they came upon it, and she supposed the church that owned the camp might demolish the bench one day. She hoped they wouldn't, because she liked the odd pairing, wondered at the mind of the stone carver who had created it.

Cal had rackets with him, a pair of birdies. She knew he had to have flown to get the rackets and be at the court before her.

He stood awkwardly, handed her a racket. She thought he wanted to say something. He looked at her but did not speak. Instead he gestured with his racket to take the court, choose her side.

She walked to one half of the mown grassy rectangle. It was a lovely court, surrounded on all sides by shrubs and hedges, some raspberry bushes. She heard the drone of bees, the hot sound of an early summer morning.

He served; they batted the birdie back and forth for practice. He asked her if she wanted to begin, and she nodded her head.

Her arm was long, and she knew how to hustle. No shot was beyond her reach, and that was her most serious flaw, going for shots that were clearly out of bounds. He played a steady game, his eye better than hers, running less, letting the long shots go, but she saw that he was playing for real, that he knew almost immediately that she could play the game, that she might beat him.

She liked the airy thwack of the birdie against the taut strings of the racket. She liked to smash it at the net, sending it to the grass before he could react. She laughed when she herself missed a shot. Once she ran backward for a high loop, the birdie vanishing in the sun, then lost her balance, tripped, fell onto the grass. He came to the net, asked if she was all right. Her shorts had grass stains in the back. She wiped them off. I'm fine, she said, laughing again, then served a brilliant shot, one she knew he would let go, would think was going over the line, and when it landed perfectly in the corner, he whistled in appreciation.

The score was 16–14, or perhaps something else, but he was winning, just. He stood poised for his serve, and she waited. He was looking at her through the net, and she thought that he was thinking about where to place his shot. He had the sleeves of his white shirt rolled above the elbows. He wore black pants, white sneakers. He held the racket and the birdie out, at arms' reach. He didn't move. She was going to goad him, then sensed something, stopped herself. All around them, there was quiet, a deep summer hush. He raised the racket and the birdie, made his serve. It was a terrible shot, she could see that at once. The birdie veered off to the side, hit the pole, ricocheted to the ground. Embarrassed for him, she ran to the place where the birdie had fallen, bent over from the waist to retrieve it. He ran to get it too, possibly apologetic. When she bent, her hair parted at her neck, fell forward over her face.

She felt it, shivered slightly.

A kiss at the nape of the neck. A butterfly.

His lips—his dry, boyish lips—made the shape of a butterfly against the back of her neck. She felt the light touch against her skin, thought, Butterfly.

She stood up, looked at him. She wanted to reach out, touch him on the arm. She wanted to take one step forward, kiss him on the cheek. She wanted to say again that it was all right to have done what they had the night before, that it was not all right that she was leaving him. She wanted to tell him that she would never forget him, no matter what happened to her.

But she could not move that one step closer. And he could not touch her. He shifted a fraction to the side, as if he would return to his half of the court. She smoothed her hair back off her face.

He said, Siân.

She meant to speak, couldn't, hesitated a fraction too long.

They turned simultaneously, took up their positions. She had the birdie; she had lost track of the score now. She thought that possibly he ought still to have possession of the birdie, but that didn't seem to matter.

She raised her racket. She would sail him a long one. She smiled, and she saw, through the net, that he was smiling back at her, in anticipation.

She hit the shot. She watched it soar into the sun.

And it seemed to her that it was then that the birdie, high above them both, stopped at its apex, stopped in time.

Appendix

Where or When

WORDS BY LORENZ HART
MUSIC BY RICHARD RODGERS

When you're awake
The things you think come from the dreams you
    dream.
Thought has wings,
And lots of things are seldom what they seem.
Sometimes you think you've lived before
All that you live today.
Things you do come back to you,
As though they knew the way.
Oh, the tricks your mind can play!

It seems we stood and talked like this before.
We looked at each other in the same way then,
But I can't remember where or when.
The clothes you're wearing are the clothes you wore.
The smile you are smiling you were smiling then,
But I can't remember where or when.

Some things that happen for the first time,
Seem to be happening again.
And so it seems that we have met before,
and laughed before,
and loved before,
But who knows where or when!

The Tape That
Charles Sent Siân

A Teenager in Love
Dion

Angel Baby
Rosie & The Originals

That's My Desire
Dion & The Belmonts

Where or When
Dion & The Belmonts

Mr. Blue
The Fleetwoods

Come Softly to Me
The Fleetwoods

What's Your Name?
Don and Juan

In the Still of the Night
The Five Satins

To Know Him Is to Love Him
The Teddy Bears

Here Comes the Night
Them

Don't Look Back
Them

Will You Love Me Tomorrow
The Shirelles

Crying
Roy Orbison

Love Hurts
Roy Orbison

Donna
Ritchie Valens